Joy Buchanan lives with her family at Fairmead Life Centre; a retreat and healing centre set in an organic orchard and smallholding in Somerset.

The Woman With No Clothes is her first book, written in 1995, kept in a drawer and taken out to be read and enjoyed by a few kind friends. One of these has pointed out that good or bad, a drawer is not much of a place to keep a story. It arrived out of the blue, presumably to be shared with others and not with socks, sarongs, gloves, handkerchiefs and pyjamas.

This book is therefore offered humbly to its readers in the hope that it will please them and with heartfelt thanks to all who have encouraged and supported its writing.

For Alan

The Woman With No Clothes

A story
by
Joy Buchanan

Fairmead Press

Fairmead Press

First published in Great Britain in 2007
by Fairmead Press

ISBN 978-0-9555159-0-3

Typeset in Palatino Text, Printed and bound in
Great Britain by St Andrews Press, Wells, Somerset.

www.fairmeadlife.co.uk

The Power of the Universe is Love
So
All that is not of Love
Will be overturned by Love
The fact that that which is not of Love
Is not Real
Is the Expressing Truth
Only Love Exists
So
That is all there is to do
BE OF LOVE

Contemplation

How many people in the history of man have been able to give a satisfactory explanation of the purpose of suffering? Who has not had their finger squashed, their hopes dashed, their sense of purpose thrown into question? Do you ask why? Who does not?

History books record the struggles that have ensued in assorted searches for power. What grim reading they make. What do they offer for our understanding of the nature of power, when we try to hinge it on fear? Is that not force? An action begetting a reaction? True power can only be hinged on true love.

The experience of fear disconnects us from our experience of truth. The truth is that our essence cannot be harmed. When we know this as truth, power lies unshakably within. How difficult then are we to manipulate, to enslave, to blind!

There is certainly plenty to show that those inflicting force by wielding the weapons of war and repression are fighting for their position to do just this. They attempt to conquer our minds, bodies and souls; but by this method it cannot be done. The story of mankind is peppered by sages who understand and can explain why this coercion is always fruitless. People have written down their given revelations and had them burned along with their living bodies. Individuals have been forced by unendurable circumstances to denounce their vision whilst others have held their view. Whole nations have been systematically crushed and scattered, some to extinction and some to return. Who knows what has been lost or delayed? Who knows what has been kept for a later time?

People have sung, danced, sculpted, planted, calculated, painted, written, contemplated and lived their truth. All around this planet in various combinations and forms, it waits in parts. It exists within each of us. Is it possible for those parts to combine, to bring a common truth into common understanding? Are those parts already in motion, combining even now? Don't people make love? Don't they teach their children? Don't they laugh? What is happening at such times if not this?

CHAPTER ONE

Mary Makes A Reflection

It is high spring, just before anyone has had time to cut the verges. Cow parsley, young nettles and buttercups lean into the narrow road. They brush against Mary's car, lush and welcoming. She feels herself go deeper in to her life. She likes the feeling. This letting go is such a relief.

She can see little beyond the high banks on either side of the road. They are topped with hedgerow, fox gloves and the bare, bulging roots of ash trees. Occasionally, a cow's head appears above her, its eyes following her passing car with gentle gaze as it browses on tender shoots. She is looking for a turning to the left, a track, but it is probably overgrown by now. Perhaps she should get past these fields and into the woodland ahead. Little birds hop off the road or swoop in front of the windscreen as she passes. Mary slows down further, eager not to cause harm. It is more than fifteen years since last she came this way, she and Tim.

As Mary scans for the turning, she simultaneously wonders what has become of him, the one who had been her first love; a time of exaltation suddenly diminished by what happened here. In her early twenties, Mary had fallen in love through the heat and drought of a summer. Then too, she had felt life vibrating in every leaf and its flow whispering to her from each tree and flower. Mary had felt so sweetly connected to the life erupting all around her in bud, tendril and scent. It lapped at her feet. It flowed through her. She was part of it, and it a part of her. She loved everything. At last, she had begun to join in and with the arrival of spring, celandines had burst out beneath her feet, as love had burst open her heart, ending two winters at once.

Then a day came when she and Tim went walking in ancient woodland. Their path had led along the ridge of an abandoned quarry, now flooded. From below them came the sound of gentle splashing. They looked down.

In the deep water a naked woman swam. Her long grey hair floated upon the surface of the water as she rested, lying back and open to the sky. Only her hands moved a little as she guided herself across the pool. She was brown from the sun, no part of her kept from its radiance. The water was clear, reflecting the blue of the sky, sparkling as the light caught it lapping against her body.

Without reference to each other, Tim and Mary stopped to gaze at her. She drifted to an overhang of rock on the other side of the quarry, turned over and reached up to pull herself out of the water. Her ascent was almost ungainly as she levered herself up.

She climbed higher still to another overhang, some five meters above the surface of the water. Her discarded clothes lay nearby; bright yellow, blue and green. The woman ignored them and walked to the edge. She began to sway from foot to foot, developing a rhythm to music that she hummed. She hummed more loudly, swaying with greater energy and beginning to lift her feet to the rhythm that she made. Then she broke into full song and began to dance with the whole of herself as she filled the amphitheatre of the quarry with her sound. It was pure joy. She lifted her arms and face to the sun-filled sky.

Her singing was rich, melodious and without inhibition. The song throbbed all around Mary who was transfixed with a longing to join this woman and to give herself to the moment as completely as she. She knew she loved, but she couldn't show it like this and she felt the richness of her own new discovery begin to pale.

The singing stopped and the woman moved right to the edge of the great rock. Taking a deep breath, she leaped deep into the water, almost vanishing. She was out of breath when she bobbed up, smiling and shaking the hair and water from her face before resuming her peaceful floating.

Mary and Tim continued their walk, stopping later while Tim made love to her, excited by the spectacle of freedom that they had witnessed. But Mary made no love. She was distracted by what she had seen. That woman in the quarry was able, somehow, to be herself. Mary wanted to know what it was that put her so at ease in the world, without reference to any body else. Her own love was not so immense after all, she concluded, and began to let it vanish. In the face of this brighter light, she could not allow it to illuminate her. Instead, she felt humiliated and that she had failed. Her sense of personal ignorance grew until, diminished by it, she belittled the love that was hers with which to grow.

The bond between Tim and Mary fizzled out. He had taken on life with even greater alacrity. Mary had locked herself away in the dark, believing that she could never be like that woman. She had disqualified herself from what she saw as 'the contest of life' before anyone else could, and took to winter again, unable to admit the simple message that had been laid before her.

In the years since that time, with work, marriage and motherhood, her search for such open-hearted living had never ceased and yet she could find no gauge by which to measure or explain away her confusion. If you reaped what you sowed, how come all the love she had given had left her feeling so empty? Her striving to fill this space by refusing nothing to others, had robbed her dry. She had not seen then that only a gift from the bottom of her heart could ever be returned by its own likeness. She had deceived herself, thinking she had gone so deep when in fact by such withholding, she had barely begun to tap that wondrous resource.

Despite the clue of thickening trees, Mary almost misses the turning. Wild honeysuckle, elder and brambles have filled the entrance. It is the break in the hawthorn that catches her eye and causes her to stop the car and reverse for a second look. She cannot drive the car through, but the break in the trees beyond shows that the track can still be followed on foot.

Mary pulls the car off the road, its wheels crushing the thick, crisp stalks of the cow parsley and squelching into red clay mud. Getting out of the car, the warm of the late morning sunshine blesses her skin through the rich blue wool of her jersey. She is wearing jeans and brown leather boots and feels so good in these things, which hang a little loose. She has brought a small picnic which is nestled beneath a towel in her basket. There is no breeze. A blackbird sings into the still air.

Picking her way through the newly exposed mud, Mary pushes through the plants that have almost hidden the track. The bramble catches on her jersey and she has to control her eagerness whilst she frees herself. She notices that her hands are shaking.

As she makes her way along the feint track, birds call out a warning to their neighbourhood as she passes. Again, Mary feels the intoxicating sensation of moving deeper into her life, of drawing closer to her self and becoming more real. As she takes each step along the path, no one could tell her for sure where it will lead. No one knows and she doesn't know either. This is her visit, her journey, her event. There is nothing to do but to surrender and this way of letting go is becoming a passion. Not needing to know is a liberation in itself. As she walks, her mind wavers between dreaminess and acute awareness as she is alternately splashed by sunshine and shade.

Then through sparse trees, she sees the water. Mary quickens her pace, leaves the track, crashes through an undergrowth of bluebells, ferns and early bracken fronds and ducks beneath low branches that whip shut behind her. A badger path, running along the edge of the quarry, leads her on. She wants to get to the rock where she saw the woman. She notices, but does not pause at the place where she and Tim had stood to watch her.

The path diverges, one leading steeply down to a drinking place for wild animals and the other loops back into the woodland. Mary takes neither. The next few steps will take her onto the summit of the great rock where the woman had danced and sung. Despite her eagerness, she slows herself to tread carefully round the edge of the quarry, balancing high above the water. Twigs crack beneath her, the sound made soft by the old, damp leaves from last autumn and the rot of a wet winter. Runners and roots catch at her feet, sending little clumps of humus bustling down the slope to her right. Then she steps across the threshold from the woodland, onto the rock.

The sun is set to shine all day. She puts down her basket and removes her boots. The rock is warm and tingles her feet. She takes off all her clothes and lies on the rock, gazing at the water below. It is still, giving clearly defined reflections of the guarding crown of trees that grow along the rim of the quarry. The sun's reflection dazzles. Mary blinks and rests her chin on her hands, folding them onto the surface of the rock. Despite the stillness, occasional ripples spread across the water. Perhaps there are fish. There are certainly insects. Each time a ripple shimmers down the reflection of the trees, Mary feels something shimmering through her. She knows this feeling now for herself. It is joy. All she has to do is to look at the water, see the light and there is joy. She does not have to bid for it, earn it, manufacture it or imagine it. It simply is in existence within the water, the light, the warmth, the rock, the trees, the sounds - within her.

All the time that has passed since her first visit and now, all the beliefs she has clung to, the life she has made to uphold them, the sheer harshness of her existence, melts away. She will never have to go back unless she chooses. Now she is ready for a bolder adventure than she could ever have previously imagined and all there is for her to do, is this - to feel the sun on her skin, to sense the living rock beneath her, to jump in to the water, cold or not.

She rolls over onto her back. May blossoms above her, creamy white against the sky. More joy. Mary pulls her picnic basket towards her, rummages inside and finds a small pie. She lies back, eating and enjoying the flakes of pasty falling down beside her. Dark musty mushrooms, goat cheese, coriander and thyme, baked for her by her brother. Next, two crisp young carrots. She lies on her side to eat these, the crunchy texture too hard to be eaten whilst her head rests on rock. Then a chunk of bread pudding, rich with peel and plump sultanas. Mary eats this sitting cross-legged, gazing out over the water again.

She has found the spot she sought. She has taken off her clothes. She has eaten the delicious and potentially distracting picnic. Now she continues to sit, easing herself forward and to the side so as to dangle her legs over the edge and gain some shade. She is joining in again. She melts into contemplation, recalling the day when the great thaw had, at last, begun.

CHAPTER TWO

War Begins At Home

Mary was unaware of the significance of her inner life and that an internal war, waged behind the shutters of her conditioning, was actually taking place and expressing itself outwardly. She hoped constantly and yet vaguely that at some point soon things would get better and then she would feel better too. In the meantime she worked hard to be good, to be perfect, to be acceptable. She put aside her longings and addressed the needs of her family as she should, but only turmoil came. Things did not seem to work out. She felt cheated, confused, wasted. Time passed.

One night, pegging out the pale family wash as the moon glared down at her, she had felt as a rabbit must when caught in the headlights of a car. Frozen in panic, Mary felt certain that she had been discovered and was being watched by some great, unknowable thing that knew all her failings and judged her to be wanting. If she was to escape such scrutiny, she must try harder, dig deeper to find those qualities that she believed she ought to possess. That would pull her through. But where was her humour, her patience, her generosity? They were, she felt, completely used up. They no longer existed within her and she could discover no resource with which to manufacture them. Mary did not know that she was disappointed with herself. She thought that she was disappointed with everyone else and oh how that lack of understanding made her rage!

Right now, after Pascal's disobedience, that rage welled up and out. She pulled him roughly from the kitchen to the bottom of the stairs, shoving him against the wall and holding him there, her arms as iron with all the frustration bursting in her joints. Throughout her body, anger fizzed, hissed and hurt her. Where the door made an angle with the wall, she pinned him into the corner. His head whip-lashed, knocking against the hard surface. His face responded in shock. She took the neck of his tee shirt with both her hands, leaning down so that their eyes were level. Her face burned next to his as she shot out her words,

"Go up! Go up now and just do it! There's nothing else! Not a single thing until it's done!" Spit flicked out on to his cheek. As she shouted, her passion increased. "I've done every thing for you! Everything! You're spoiling my day. You're spoiling Jenny's day!"

"And you're spoiling my day!" He was crying. His eyes looked back, brimming and spilling with tears, piercing through her rage to touch the depths of her love for him. In those moments such a range of thoughts was possible that she felt shocked by them. She thought of the things that she had planned to do today. Images of her shopping, walking the dogs, completing paperwork all flashed across her inner eye, yet for the moment she was dealing with this, and she was jolted back to this painful and noisy confrontation.

Despite their eye contact and the chance of restraint that it offered, the performance continued, fuelled by its own momentum. Besides, the fury continued to surge through her, sweeping aside the chance to stop and do this in a different way.

"Don't you dare accuse me!" she shouted. "Don't you dare!" There was no place in her mind where she could put herself on trial for this in addition to everything else. "This is entirely your fault! If you just got on with it, everyone else would be happy!" Still clutching his shirt, she yanked him towards her and then, changing her grip to hold his upper arms, she propelled him up the stairs. She squeezed his arms tightly as tension ran into her hands.

Even then his own sense of outrage gave him the strength to go slowly, looking back and down upon her, showing his hurt and despair and his wish for revenge.

Mary went back to the kitchen, the sink, the washing up, the little soggy messes of tea leaf and sodden crust. She felt overwhelmed by such extremity of feeling. Was that really what it took to get her son to start his homework? She laughed cynically at herself. It wasn't over yet. All that had been achieved by the row was that Pascal had gone up some stairs. What he was now doing was unknown. She would have to go and see when she was calmer.

Mary felt a lump of misery hurting her throat. It was raw from all the shouting and she had difficulty swallowing. Shame was burning deep inside. Her hands trembled as she washed the china cups and with an unsteady clatter, put them to drain. Her hands seemed to be far away and slightly out of her control.

A further wave of impatience flowed through her. She felt the snare of the inertia she so feared, tighten. She looked around at all the undone things, left while she had fought with Pascal. And for what? It wasn't her fight, it was a proxy fight. Somehow by becoming a mother, she seemed to have become lost between her ideal and the compelling weight of her society and its muddled requirements. Here in her own home, sanctuary from a deaf and blundering world, she had fought in its favour against her own son and not for the first time. Would she do it again? How could she stop it?

Mary looked out of the kitchen window. Her hair, shoved into a tired little ponytail in the rush of the morning, was coming loose. Strands hung around her face, tickling her nose and cheeks. Her hands wet, she rubbed her face against her upper arm and the matted wool of her old, pale green jersey. Out on the lawn she could see Jenny and her friend Myra by the swing. Myra lay across it, her tummy on the seat. She was hanging limply, scraping the toes of her pink wellington boots in the mud as Jenny pushed her. Jenny was counting, or was she singing? Without her glasses, Mary could not see. She squinted. Jenny finished, and clapped her hands. Myra came to life and jumped up. The girls swapped places, the chill breeze whisking Jenny's dark hair against the slipstream of the swinging.

To the side of the swing, lilac bushes grew and in the wind the blooms bounced at the ends of their branches. They reminded Mary of what she felt unable to do - to bounce back, to pull her socks up, to get back on the horse after a fall. She could understand the principle, but she had fallen off so many times that she was bruised, muddied, maybe even broken. She probably didn't deserve another go.

She felt utterly at sea. She pictured herself in some sort of boat. It was small, clinker built and although once painted bright blue it was now shabby. The sea was choppy and she was being tossed about. If there were any oars she could not see them and besides, she was using her hands to hold on and could not spare them for rowing. In the distance, dark cliffs rose out of the water. There were no other boats in sight. No help. All she could do, all she could think of, was to hold on tight.

Yesterday morning after the usual chaos of preparing for the journey to school, pins of adrenalin had run through her all the way. Yet again she had had to dress Pascal, pour his cereal, butter his toast, gather his school things and force him into the car. Jenny had managed everything for herself and now Mary cringed to recall how little she had praised her.

In the car, Pascal had sat dejected in the back. Mary had put him there where he could not reach the doors. She and Jenny had sung together and arrived cheerfully at school. For Mary, this was the outer layer, the front that she presented to the world, contrived, false but, she hoped, convincing. The sickening turmoil inside went on. She was worried about where to park. She was worried about having to talk to people. She was worried in case Pascal refused to get out of the car, or walk through the gates, or into the classroom.

She saw the parental friendship groups engaged in light, morning chatter. They seemed relaxed, in charge, exclusive. Their children grouped up and walked happily into school, parting from their mothers with a quick kiss or casual wave of a hand. These women didn't seem to notice their own children. Mary noticed hers. She had shown hers how to sing, although Pascal only sang on the way home. She had wanted Jenny to be noticed, singing with her, her mother. As they had pulled into the school, Mary had made a particular point of starting another verse to ensure that the song would last to the stop. Now, with her hands dripping with the cooling water and dying suds, she was distressed by this recollection of her singing as an act of aggression. She had wanted to show that she was the best mother, the one who was the most fun, but probably, if anyone had noticed her at all, she had just looked like a silly, eccentric woman.

This bleak glimpse exposed a shift in her heart. What had happened that she was beginning to compete in this way? When had the cut gone so deep that she needed to push people away instead of showing kindness? Since Pascal had started school, her dreams of helping him through, backing up his school work, having a fruitful rapport with his teacher, expanding her group of friends had, one by one, been dashed. Pascal didn't fit in and neither did she. She wanted to live fully, but her life felt as if it had gone onto hold. Jenny had her own extraordinary self-possession and know-how. She found her way through despite her mother and brother. Mary felt needy and wanted a friend who was willing to share all this and help her to understand. If she could, would she start to grow again?

She finished the washing-up and let out the water, turning to dry her hands on the threadbare, beige roller towel. She looked at her watch. It was already late morning and so little achieved! She must go and see Pascal and start reconciliation. She made sugary tea and took some biscuits from the tin. What about a little vase of flowers? No! Crazy, smothering idea! This tray was enough. She had been wrong to let the anger swamp her so, although she could not help it.

As Mary went to the stairs, Jenny ran into the hallway, laughing with Myra. She fell against Mary, knocking the little tray from her hands. The mug of tea went flying against the wall before smashing down onto the plate and biscuits which had broken on the tiled floor. The wall darkened as the tea soaked in to it. This was the very spot where rage had so recently had free rein. Chaos still lingered there.

Jenny and Myra were transfixed. They were inclined to apologise but were unsure whether it wouldn't be safer to invest in defence, rushing into claims that found fault outside their sphere of friendship. In the pause, Mary saw and understood their doubts, taking to her heart their fear of her unpredictability. On the edges of their fear, she wavered, experiencing for herself a feeling of power and a desire to indulge it. She could inflict blame, bestow forgiveness, delegate clearing up and, in any one of these cases, rob the girls of an opportunity to offer their own solutions.

"How shall we put this right?" she asked, feeling magnanimous. She noted the relief on their faces.

The girls went to get a dustpan, brush and a bucket of soapy water, but on opening the door to the kitchen, the dogs rushed forward. Thinking only of their stomachs, but not of broken china, they had heard the crash and were coming through to check it out.

"Out! Out!" chorused Mary and Jenny. Their shouting bewildered the dogs who, sensing that time to explore was likely to come to an abrupt halt, eagerly poked their noses closer to danger. Myra, unused to dogs or shouting, became confused and shut the kitchen door. Three dogs now frantically milled around, unable to leave. Bingo, keen to eat at any price, snapped desperately at the mess of biscuits before Jenny or Mary could grab her collar and stop her. She yelped in pain as she was cut. Blood began to stain her dribble.

Roger and Walrus whined and barked as someone knocked on the door. Two large envelopes plopped through the letter-box. The knock came again, encouraging the dogs to renew their efforts. Walrus began her leaping trick, jumping up to the high, glass section on the front door and attempting to see who was there. Months of this behaviour had marked the paintwork with a vertical patch of scratches and paw smudges. Mary bent down and put her mouth to the letter-box.

"Please just leave it on the doorstep, it's a bit busy in here," she called. The postman stayed. He was saying something, but she couldn't hear him. She craned her ear to the letter-box. Walrus, putting her great paws on to Mary's back, tried to lever herself up, whining loudly.

Suddenly, something pointed came through the slot into Mary's ear. She jerked her head away just in time to catch Walrus's wet nose on the other side of her head. Instinctively, she recoiled from the cold nose, banging her head back against the door.

The postman was trying to get Mary's signature by posting a pen and recorded delivery form into the house. Mary, crouching into a ball on the floor, with her back to the broken china, bleeding dog and agitated children, made a sort of tent with her body. She signed, then used the biro to try to lever open the letter box, but it snapped. Still kneeling, she opened the door a crack in order to return the broken pen and paper. Walrus jumped onto her back and snarled through the crack above her head. Roger sniffed loudly through the crack below her head. Bingo continued to whine in the background as Jenny and Myra called to them all to try to urge them away.

Mary felt laughter begin to leap up inside her. She peered through the gap, her eyes twinkling. She slotted the papers and pen back to the postman who handed her a fat envelope.

"Thank you," said Mary, hoping that he might see how she wanted to laugh with another adult. If he did, he wasn't going to join her. He always had a serious bearing and it was difficult to raise a smile from him, but today, with all this? Wasn't this just a bit funny, something to share? Mary felt foolish as he walked away down the path. "Sorry about the pen!" she called, as he swung the gate shut and drove off.

Now, only moments after she had wanted to laugh and laugh to exhaustion, she felt that she might cry. She pushed the door shut and leaned against it, still sitting on the floor. Walrus, now quiet, nosed at her in love as she drew in her breath. Her skirt and jersey were crumpled, hitched up, dog haired and dusty. A shaft of sunshine beamed in through the door, lighting up the dust motes that floated abundantly around her. By the skirting board, clumps of felted house dust whispered and scuttled before settling back behind the hat stand, the plant stand, the umbrella stand and hall chair. All was still.

The girls gazed at Mary. Bingo had stopped bleeding and sat on the bottom stair, affronted. Mary sighed again. She gazed at the letter in her hand. It was only the usual weekly letter from Bruce's mother.

"Come on. Let's have another go at sorting this out," said Mary. She felt weak and even a little giddy as she struggled to her feet. With her hands, she brushed and smoothed down her colourless, shapeless clothes.

CHAPTER THREE

The Obscurity Of Peace

As soon as she could, Mary made more tea to take up to Pascal. She noticed with unease that an hour and a half had passed since their quarrel. As she went up to him, her heart was sinking. The stairwell was cold. Under the old, brown carpet, the stair boards creaked. Bare plaster awaiting redecoration seemed to suck in the light, emphasizing the gloomy feel that was unrelieved by the dim, ecological light bulb hanging from a wire above her. Steam rose from the mug as if to increase the bleakness.

"I am warm right through, unlike you," it quite clearly said.

"But I want to be warm right through," she replied. "I'm a warm hearted person, full of love and life, humour and spontaneity. It's just that doing all this has made me spring a leak and everything has drained out. See the way I come up these stairs? I'm puffing for air and dragging my feet and so would you if you were me." She felt her feet, weighty in her shoes, dangling from her ankles before she placed them onto each step.

At the top she stood appalled at the sound coming from Pascal's room. After all this time he was still weeping. She felt her heart twist and saliva leapt from under her tongue. She felt angry too. How could he have not given in? If he had at least made a start, there would be a chance for joy in the day.

Mary pushed open the door. Pascal tried to increase his volume as he continued to take revenge, but he was close to exhaustion. He had become completely incapable of doing anything. His voice cracked into hoarseness. He was lying curled up on the floor and now put his arms around his head, reminding Mary of how she had defended herself to write for the postman. Pascal's school books lay about the room, battered and loathed, but intact. A pencil, one that Father Christmas had brought two years ago, was splintered beneath the desk.

'The day of the broken writing implements,' Mary thought, wondering how in the midst of all this distress, she could think so ironically. She looked at her adored son. She could not understand why this kept happening. She and Bruce, muddled as they were about some things, really had been consistent in this aspect of their parenting, although Bruce more by principle than by action. They had agreed that if Pascal had homework, then he would have to do it. In their different ways, they were intelligent, imaginative people. They were responsible parents. She had tried everything, yet the harvest was barren. In fact, it was worse than barren. It was a pestilence which had invaded the whole of their family life. Everything she tried or wanted to do was infected by the blight. Their home was contaminated. Each family member suffered and here, at the centre of it, lay Pascal with his stubborn will.

Mystified by the scale of her sudden furies towards Pascal, she did not guess that such passionate rages were inversions of her love. What could explain them? The fact that they may have their birth in a lack of love for herself, was not in her current power to consider. She believed that she was ruining Pascal's life and thought only in terms of what she should be or do for him.

On the desk, heaps of pencil shavings were mingled with paper-clips, bits of wool and tiny, bright plastic pegs. Yesterday, Mary had cleared and polished this surface, hoping as she did so that the desk would look inviting and help to avoid the miserable sort of time that they were now having. She pushed the mug against the mess and set it down before kneeling by her sobbing child. She wanted to hold him. She lay down beside him, curving her body round his, all hot and cold at once. She put her arms around him, stroking his upper arm and shoulder. For a while she said nothing, then, running her fingers through his hair, she asked,

"What are we to do about all this?" Pascal had stopped crying, but his breath still came shakily. His face, buried for so long in anguish and wet with tears, was pale, blotched with harsh red.

"I don't know. I don't know. It's stupid. I can't do any of it."

"You can't if you won't try. You have to try."

"Why? It's all pointless and boring. It's no good. It's too difficult."

"If it's difficult, let me help you."

"No. You just get cross. You say you won't, but you do."

This truth made panic flutter in Mary's breast. She couldn't bear to hear it because it was so exactly opposite to all that she strived to achieve. She had invested everything in motherhood and here was undeniable evidence that she had failed supremely. Her own childhood had been difficult - whose, indeed had not? School had been something to muddle through, and muddle was the operative word here as she strove to survive in a confusing world that seemed to know something that she did not.

Through all of this, she had held a thread of hope. It was to do with love. She wanted love to be the greatest power in existence, but life did not seem to bear this out. She held this hope right down inside herself, a secret not to be exposed. She had not even told Bruce. She had reckoned that when at last she had a child of her own, she would be able to prove it.

Now this seemed impossible. Scorn waited close by in the wings, hissing and booing at each moment of failure, scattering this central hope of her life.

It frightened her to discover herself to be so weak. The expectation was that Pascal would participate with school, yet she could see how much he hated it. She had tried to talk it over with the school, with Bruce, with friends, with her parents, but none of them seemed concerned by his distress. It was viewed by all but her as a matter of holding firm against Pascal's resistance, which would ultimately lead to him seeing that he must knuckle down like the rest of the children. Further exploration was not encouraged. Who was she to question that weight of opinion?

"Pascal, you know you have to do this. Everyone finds they have to do things they don't much like. Why not just get on with it, get it out of the way. Just do it." Her voice took on a sharper edge as the panic flared again. Pascal moved away. Under the bed, fluff mingled with marbles, lego and some forgotten knitting.

"I've brought you some sweet tea." She got up to reach for it and handed it to Pascal. They sat together on the floor in the midst of their armistice.

CHAPTER FOUR
The Busy Breadwinner

In his restaurant kitchen, Bruce was baking as he approached the busiest part of his day. His floured hands and forearms delved into the huge, metal mixing bowl as he gathered the dough that he had made. He stood on a step to give him height for this work, reaching down into the basin to knead. As well as his apron, his shirt, jeans and beard were dusted with flour. Around him his staff bustled, making up orders, clearing and cleaning tables or loading the dishwasher. Voices calling details of food orders, making observations, teasing and sometimes complaining, rose and fell above the clatter.

In this area of the city, lunches and teas were wanted. By evening, everything became quiet. Bruce had only occasionally flirted with the possibility of keeping open after seven o'clock.

From noon onwards, High Table served lavish high teas. Customers could sit at small, intimate tables or if they wished, they could join others on the larger ones. The more people round a table the less per head they had to pay. When at work, Bruce was a cheerful and sunny soul and he had brought his personality flooding into the restaurant, putting all comers at their ease. The idea had flourished as over the years he had gained a reputation for helping people to relax and venture, although strangers at first, to eat together.

The tables were round, with bright blue cotton cloths and multi-coloured napkins. The food came in a way that demanded communication between all the people at each table. The cakes were varied, unlabeled and uncut. Tea came in large pots and needed to be poured, along with jugs of milk and cream, pats of butter and jars of jam. Because they had to speak about the food, the ice of unfamiliarity was easily broken and smiles soon followed.

The restaurant swung from running smoothly, to there being sudden hitches without apparent warning. A person apparently content on Tuesday would hand in their notice on Wednesday. Bruce did not try to understand these changes, they just happened; but this wasn't his way. The thought of drifting and never seeming to get your teeth into anything, simply didn't appeal to him. He liked a challenge, but he also liked to know where he was, to have a sense of purpose and direction. Then he could reflect and get a sense of progress, or not.

Bruce liked to feel that his life showed progress. He secretly rather despised people who took pride in not changing. It was one thing for life just to happen not to change, but quite another to make a point of holding it fast and drawing attention to this as if it were a virtue. Self-promotion at the expense of others annoyed him very much; the habit some people had of comparing themselves favourably to others about whose lives and choices they knew nothing. It was so presumptuous. He had two customers, in particular, who were like this. There was Clive and there was Marjory, the poor old thing. In fact apart from Mandrake, they were the only two for whom he had to make an effort. Everyone else was easy enough.

Sometimes a group of people in some sort of difficulty would arrive. They might have someone fractious with them. They might be tired from shopping or be initially unaware of the unusual nature of his establishment. All of these people Bruce enjoyed easing into the fun of the place, even if as sometimes happened, they took out their worries on him. Worries came in many forms. Rudeness was common. Being indecisive about where to sit or what to eat was another. The one that amused him the most, perhaps because he was used to it both in his mother and his wife, was that of appearing unable to understand any information. It required a lot of attention and repetition to help people like that to relent and allow comforts to be given.

These people and the situations they brought made the days colourful. Clive and Marjory however, taxed him with their smug attachment to themselves. He had first noticed

Clive in the quiet of a mid-week pub, engaging the bar-tender in talk about the new traffic system then being constructed in the city. Bruce had kept his distance recognizing this as a trapping and boring conversation. He had rather disliked himself for lingering within earshot in order that he could go home and sneer about it with Mary. He hoped that he would never get caught by this lifeless man.

That was back in the days when he was running the contract cleaning at the city hospital. Clive had surprised him by turning up as a porter there, within two weeks of the eavesdropping. Bruce noticed, his attention caught in passing, that Clive was rather good at his job and seemed to have learned the ropes quickly. When helping to transport patients, he didn't have time to bore them. In fact, he cheered them up with his uninhibited chatter.

On his supervision rounds, Bruce would call into the porter's lodge for a catch-up. If Clive was there, he would be holding the floor with his talking, seemingly unaware of the effect on others as he espoused his cause, usually along the theme of 'reasons why I am wise to resist change'. Proposed evidence would then follow, along with exhaled cigarette smoke. Bruce would feel repulsed by Clive's sallow skin and the hint of dandruff in his lank hair. He also felt confusion because Clive seemed so able and yet he boastfully clung to the past, distancing himself with the traits of a loner. Loner or not, when he was at High Table at the same time as his children, Jenny and Pascal both seemed to like him. He always gave them the time of day.

When Bruce pulled out of the cleaning business and set up High Table, of all his hospital contacts it was Clive who had come to the opening. He still came to the restaurant and at each meeting, because of his subsequent dark thoughts, Bruce was reminded of his own ungenerous nature.

After mulling over his thoughts about Clive, Bruce was in the habit of then moving on to Marjory. As he knocked today's breads and cakes from their tins onto the cooling trays, he moved into his Marjory appraising mode. He was homing in on one of his favourite memories of her, rather enjoying a gloating feeling rising inside him, when he caught his bare hand against the oven door, snatched it away and sent a tray of rock buns and scones scuttling across the floor. In the same moment that he cursed his fate, he also recognised the warning, probably from God. He liked to think he knew better than to engage in mean thoughts, yet he still liked doing it.

Bruce set about clearing up the cakes. They would be enjoyed by his dogs later. For now, there was just enough time to make some more. As he worked he resolved that he would reflect on something better than before and stir those thoughts into the mixture. He resolved, as he had many times before, to live an exemplary life.

CHAPTER FIVE

Unruly Hair and People

At the city hospital Clive was having his lunch break, sitting on a low brick wall in the car park. A gentle breeze played tricks with his hair. Clive used his hair to play tricks on himself. He had trained a long swag to cover up his baldness. In the mornings, he averted his eyes from the mirror until he had a brush in his hands, ready to sweep it over his pate, pulling the hair across with it. He never put on his glasses until after he had created the impression he wanted. Without them, his blurred vision conveyed a man with a full head of hair. Sometimes he contemplated coming clean with himself, going to the barber and having the swag taken away, but when his thoughts turned in this direction, he got an image of himself, standing in front of his bathroom mirror without it. The prospect made him curl up inside. He couldn't do it, not yet.

Now the wind was picking it up and flicking it over his eyes and then dying down, leaving it in his face and forcing Clive to deal with it, to clear it away. No sooner had he done this, than the wind would rise again and whisk it out of place. Clive tried not to think of how he must look, but the wind made this difficult, it being so persistent in repeating the game.

Behind him grew little trees, their pink blossoms now rapidly fading and falling. The wind brought the petals down into his lap, on to his head and his sandwich. He liked these trees and the little spiky ground cover plants that grew evergreen beneath them. He remembered when the hospital had been built and the trees planted soon after, softening the hard lines of the tarmac, concrete and glass.

The trees had thrived there and he had helped them. When they were about two years old, before he had even come to work at the hospital, he had noticed them when he was at home on shore-leave. Walking to the pub one wintery evening, he took a short-cut through the car park, turning his jacket collar against the cold and hunching his shoulders in chilled tension. His hands were chapped, clenched in his pockets and irritated by the cold of his keys and coins. His feet were damp, his cheap trainers suddenly seeming to be poor value in England in November.

A group of about ten youngsters were hanging around. They were talking loudly to one another, giving off a feeling that could make you unsettled if you didn't know your way around the world.

One of them began to pull at a young tree. Clive could tell that it wouldn't be long before they were all copying, putting the saplings at risk.

"Achtung!" Clive called for their attention. He often used his basic German if he thought he could get away with it. In situations such as this, it could throw people off their guard and give him the advantage. The boys shifted uneasily at his approach. Most of them looked down, shuffling dead leaves with their feet. Street lamps cast orange light onto the wet tarmac, the soggy leaves and litter. The leader scowled, trying to look cool, but he was obviously nervous. "Leave it," said Clive, faking a German accent. The group encircled him, leaning in at him. One of them began to jeeringly chant the words of a current song, something about death, and the others joined in giving a slow hand clap. "They're just kids," Clive thought to himself, feeling scared. Then one of them lit a firework, then another, throwing them up into the air before the gang ran off. Clive had stood up to them and now the trees gave him shade.

Today, mid-spring, Clive was working for the operating theatres which usually required him to take bits and pieces from theatre to the pathology laboratory. Most specimens were impossible for him to identify, just pieces of bloody tissue in containers. But something extraordinary had had to be taken by him this morning. It was a leg, cut from below someone's knee and put into a see-through plastic bag.

The toes were black, with yellow, crusty rot in places. Just a glance sufficed to see all that. The heel had a hole in it. The shin was grossly discoloured from blue to black to raw, angry red. Only towards where the knee had been did the skin look at all normal. He was thankful that there was no knee.

He knew that people still lost their limbs these days and therefore some amputations would take place in this hospital. It wasn't the fact of the leg that was extraordinary. It was the clear bag that he had found so hard. He wondered at the indiscretion of it. It was obviously a man's leg. He had had to make his way with it, past visitors even, all the way to pathology. He thought that if it had been his leg, he would have wanted it to have more privacy than that.

When it had been handed over the red line that divided the sterility of theatre from the rest of the world, the nurse had even made a joke,

"Just hop along to path with this, will you?" she had said. A theatre technician had laughed uncertainly. Clive had wanted to cover the leg, but just as the technician had not stood up to the nurse, so he did not stand up for the leg.

"Oh no!" he exclaimed, his mouth full of sandwich, perhaps the nurse had not meant to joke, but had simply been careless with her words, exactly like him just now.

CHAPTER SIX

Fun In The Attic

That morning, Jenny had not heard Mummy and Pascal fighting. Perhaps they had done it while she and Myra were out in the garden on the swing. She knew that something had happened though. Mummy had a way of being all squashy and limp that gave it away. She had hated all the chaos after the spilt tea, with the dogs and the postman making it worse. It was embarrassing to have it happen like that, in front of a friend, especially a new one.

As soon as they could get away after all the clearing up, with Mummy sounding patient but being flappy, they had gone up to the attic to look through the old boxes. Jenny had lured Myra to come and play with the promise of doing some detective work up there. Myra was new in school this term and there was a bit of jostling going on to see who could be her friend. By implying that there was something suspicious in the attic, Jenny had assured Myra's interest and then, a visit.

Getting into the attic was tricky. There was a trap door in the ceiling of her parent's room which had to be pushed open with a pole. For two small girls, its weight and length were almost uncontrollable and they urgently whispered instructions to each other, trying to prevent it from lurching against the wallpaper or central light and causing damage they would be unable to deny. They heaved up until the counter-balance took over and swung open the door.

Next, an awkward ladder had to be pulled down with a hook that was stuck onto the far end of the pole. Jenny rightly anticipated that a shower of attic debris would fall onto the bedroom floor. A mixture of dead insects, wood lice and grit showered down onto the carpet and the end of Bruce and Mary's bed. This was sure to be provoking to them, but for now, comments about the mess or warnings of pinched fingers or ladders crashing onto heads were unlikely. Mummy and Pascal were in his room having a lull. Even if she heard the noises Mummy wouldn't come out and stop them.

Sometimes, when Mummy and Pascal were fighting, Jenny felt glad. She could do things like this without interruption. At other times she felt frightened and lonely and even though they were so angry with each other, she somehow felt left out. Who cared about her or even noticed her? She wasn't supposed to go into the attic, but in the light of what Pascal was or was not doing, the rule had disappeared. Did that mean that how she behaved, didn't matter much after all?

In the attic, Jenny put on the light. They looked about. The corners were shadowed by the junk and boxes piled across the rafters. Jenny thought that Myra looked a bit scared. It pleased her to know that something that she was arranging was having an effect on another. They stood above the ladder on a small boarded area.

"Be really careful where you step," said Jenny. "You must only tread on those plank things, otherwise you'll fall through the ceiling and there'll be trouble." Myra tensed a little more. "Come on," said Jenny and they stepped off the boards.

The air, warmed from the spring sunshine, was stuffy, smelling of camphor and dust. Between the rafters, the top side of the ceilings showed dry wooden slats with plaster squidged up through them and now coated in years of settled dirt. The light was poor.

"What's this?" asked Myra, lifting a dust sheet that covered a tall, irregular shape. Jenny looked underneath.

"That belonged to my granny. It's a sewing machine." They pulled off the cover. The smell of old oil merged into the airless space. Myra turned a small wheel. It was stiff so she used her spare hand to brace herself. "Look out!" cried Jenny, pulling Myra's hand away as the machine plunged down its needle. Myra flushed with shock. "Look," said Jenny, "this is the best way to make it go." She knelt down under the table to the treadle. Leaning onto it, she slowly swung it in to action, using the weight of her body. "Stand back!" she commanded.

As the treadle rocked back and forth, the wheel on the machine turned and the needle was set in motion. Up and down it went, faster and faster. Despite its abandonment in the attic, some parts of the machine remained shiny. They flickered as it spun, the bobbin darting back and forth like a tiny, trapped fish.

"Me! Me now!" cried Myra. She perched herself on a rafter and put her feet on the treadle. She began to peddle, lifting herself up on her hands to throw her weight forward.

"Peddle to John O' Groats and back!" shouted Jenny, above the whirring of the machine. "Go! Go!" Myra peddled faster.

"I'm going down a hill!" She slowed up. "I'm going up a mountain. It's very steep. I'm nearly there. I've made it!" Jenny clapped her.

"Now you can freewheel all the way back!" They were breathless by the time Myra returned.

"What do you want to look at now?" Jenny asked.

"Let's go along there," said Myra, pointing along a makeshift gangway between the piles. "It's like a kind of tunnel."

Carefully, the girls stepped along the beams, glancing with only mild interest at the boxes, stacks of books and clutter alongside them. Near the end, some old clothes hung in swathes from the rafters, blocking the way forward. When Myra pushed them, strands of cobweb fell to dangle and scatter dust in her face. She drew back.

"Go on!" Jenny prompted. "Let's go through."

"It's yucky," Myra protested as she turned back.

"Let me," said Jenny, squeezing past her friend. When she reached the far side of the clothes, their bulk shut out the electric light. It was too dark to see anything.

"What's it like?" called Myra.

"I can't see." Jenny checked her balance and then reached out to feel her surroundings. A few tiny chinks of light between the roof tiles began to afford light as her eyes adjusted. Right up against the gable end of the house, there lay a dark box. "I've found something, Myra! Come on!" she called.

"No! I can't! Come out. I want to go back down!" Jenny wanted to stay. She had never been this far before.

"Just a minute," she said, moving closer to the box. Now she could see it more clearly. It was not a box but a chest. Its curved top was coated in dry dirt. It was locked shut with a sort of padlock. Turning it to the light on its axis, it seemed to have no keyhole, but she could just make out engravings of twirls and stars on either side. Jenny grasped the handles at each end and tried to lift. It was too heavy for her. When she touched it, she felt so excited that her fingers tingled.

"Come on! I'm scared." Jenny jumped at the sound of Myra's voice. She had been in another world.

"Coming," she said, turning reluctantly from her find to grope her way back through the clothes. Joining Myra, the attic looked ordinary. Myra was relieved to see her.

"What are you two up to?" The question startled them both. Mummy was half-way up the ladder, trying to see them in the dim light. Spontaneously, the girls crouched down.

"Come on. I know you're there," she continued. "It's lunch time. Please don't be long and give yourselves a wash on the way down. It's pasta and tuna and things." Her head disappeared and they could hear her clanking down the last few steps.

"Phew!" exclaimed the girls, not knowing quite why - something to do with not wanting to explain and lose the magic. They went to wash, giggling at their filthy reflections in the mirror.

CHAPTER SEVEN

Bruce Rescues

At High Table, lunchtime was exceptionally busy. The atmosphere was humming with a crowd in from the nearby soft furnishings warehouse. They often came when there was something that they wanted to celebrate. Today it was Andy's birthday and they were having fun watching him decorating his cake.

This was another idea that Bruce had had, which combined increasing communication amongst his customers with pure enjoyment. For a little advance notice, he could supply a plainly iced cake and a selection of decorations, including candles. Now Andy's party was laughing together as he played around with his cake. Soon the candles would be lit and his friends would sing to him.

As he passed to and fro by the tables, Bruce could not see exactly what Andy was doing, although he could hear the laughter that his decorating was causing. The sight of people celebrating together always touched him.

The sun, bright in the blue spring sky, shone into the restaurant. Everyone responded to this, further eased into light-heartedness, noticing perhaps, if not mentioning, the hair halos on those with their backs to the window. This glorious light fell onto the display of fresh fruit on the counter, enhancing the rosy glow of the apples, the sharp green of a lime and the mellow bananas.

As he carried a batch of fairy cakes to the large central table with their brightly coloured icings rioting on the plate, Bruce felt joy in his heart. On returning to the kitchen, he paused in the doorway and turned to watch his customers. He treasured this moment, so unique and yet like so many others. How did it feel? Well organised? Running like clockwork? His own creation? A worthwhile thing anyway.

"This is a good thing," he said out loud, the lump in his throat beginning to ease.

"What?" asked Gemma as she brushed past, carrying a tray of welsh rarebits and a poached egg.

"I was just thinking," replied Bruce, "of how people all over the world have their own ways of showing their sense of community. They have all sorts of festivals, customs and gatherings when they share and support one another through life's journey. They rejoice together and they mourn together and that's what we've got going on right here."

"Ah. Hmm. Whatever," Gemma responded, fearing that the food and the egg, in particular, would get cold and anyway, what was Bruce on about now? When you had a home to run on your own and four children, there wasn't much time for such fanciful thoughts. She swept off to serve.

"I was thinking," Bruce added to no one in particular and then faltered due to the lack of a listener. Then Gemma returned and hesitated as he caught her eye. "I was thinking," Bruce said as they continued into the kitchen, "that in every community throughout the world, each uniquely expresses our commonality. It's a kaleidoscopic picture saying one thing in many ways. The more ways, the more fascinating the picture." Gemma looked at his animated face and was amused. She laughed a little as she loaded the next tray, looking across the kitchen at him. Suddenly, his face changed and seemed cast in shadow. Bruce had liked his thought of the kaleidoscope, but then his heart dipped in anxiety, mindful of how this picture was impoverished each time a culture, a way of life was destroyed. He thought of the White Witch in 'The Lion, The Witch and The Wardrobe' who, with her chilling magic, had turned a little Christmas party into stone. Gemma swept back.

"More punters!" she called, as she went out of the kitchen, nodding towards the entrance as a family came in.

"Don't call them that!" Bruce cried after her, as she went to greet and seat them.

At closing time, just as Bruce was locking up and dimming the lights, there came a sudden hammering at the door. The glass rattled harshly. A man stood there, his face in shadow from the fading light as the sun dropped behind the buildings. Bruce hung back although he recognised the man as Mandrake and knew that he had been seen. He would have to open the door or he would begin to shout. Seeing Mandrake, being with him, even just having the thought of him cross his mind always felt like the last straw. He was an unsettling man who left a trail of turbulence wherever he went.

Bruce recalled that time when he had seen Mandrake fighting in the High Street after closing time. It had been quick and messy with both men drawing blood before being separated. Bruce realised at the time that in such circumstances, he would loose badly. He would be beaten to a pulp. He put his trust in 'being nice' which was all very well if he was with people who understood the language of nice. He knew it would be no use at all in the presence of physical violence.

When Bruce and Mary had bought Mandrake's house, the chaos of his life had permeated every room. When they went to look at it for the first time, they knew in their bones as they walked across the threshold, that the house wanted them to come. Beyond the disorder, the atmosphere was of an ancient calm and it was this that called them. Above that, there was a clamouring and a misery. The clamouring was from the house, begging to be freed from the misery of having to contain such a confused being as Mandrake. When they had moved in six months ago, the house was chilled through. It had seemed to sigh with relief, although something of its former darkness, clung.

The rich, late autumn light had been striking that day. In the morning, Pascal, Jenny and the dogs had played together in their old garden for the last time. They had been throwing fallen leaves, fringed with crystals of frost. Bruce particularly remembered it because he and Mary had leaned out on the kitchen window-sill, watching them all together in the garden. They had pointed out to each other the things that they most admired. The colours were brilliant; white frost, yellow leaves, blue sky, black dogs and rosy, sparkling children. Mary had enjoyed the clarity of sound and colour. Bruce had delighted in the playfulness.

He recalled the dampened feeling they had all experienced on arrival at Stonelea. Mandrake had gone, leaving the front door ajar. Leaves had blown into the hallway and lay scattered along the chipped and displaced floor-tiles. The walls, with moistened, peeling shreds of dull green paint, seemed unaccountably cold. Upstairs, although the sun was shining at the bay windows, the mould and dirt on them seemed to make the warmth of it stop short, leaving only a watery light to trickle in.

The children had run about, shouting to make echoes fall from the ceilings to the bare, splintering floor boards and up the walls. Bruce and Mary had crept round the house in the quiet before the removal van arrived, looking at their new domain with apprehension. Their plans for Stonelea, so delightful in their previous, cosy home, suddenly seemed over ambitious or even unattainable.

On the kitchen floor, weighted down by a burned and broken cast-iron pan, lay a note. 'No forwarding address. Mandrake.' They wondered how long he had been gone.

Since that day, they had begun to work their way from room to room cleaning, decorating, carpeting and furnishing. There was still some way to go, of course. They were working on the hall and landing at the moment, a complex task that Mary wasn't getting on with as he had hoped. They were certainly making an impression and bringing their home to life, although sometimes it seemed to be touch and go as to whether they would succeed in cheering up the house, or whether it would depress them. What kind of life had Mandrake lived in it to bring it down so far?

And here was Mandrake now, glaring into the restaurant. It was the first time that Bruce had seen him since the time of the house purchase. He went over to the door and slid back the bolt. Mandrake shoved the door open and strode straight to the kitchen. When he saw Gemma washing up, he came out again and went to the counter, crouching behind it. His black anorak rustled as he squatted. His knees bulged out of gaping holes in his filthy jeans. He beckoned to Bruce who noticed that although they were looking at each other, Mandrake did not seem to be focusing.

"I'm hungry. I'm thirsty," he rasped. Bruce gave him sandwiches, cake and cold sardines on toast. He gave him warm tea and juice. Mandrake ate without inhibition. He was very dirty and the smell of him was repulsive, spreading steadily in to the restaurant and making Bruce surreptitiously check the soles of his shoes. As he leaned over his food, Bruce noticed how his thinning, dark hair revealed grit and soot against the pale skin on the top of his head.

'He's guzzling,' thought Bruce. 'I've got a guzzler in my restaurant, behind my counter, eating my left-overs. A dirty guzzler who is contravening the hygiene regulations. What provision does the Health and Safety Executive make for the unexpected guzzler being fed by a proprietor because he is both compassionate and fearful?' Mandrake looked up.

"I've been away," he said. His voice caught in his throat. He tried to clear it by giving little coughs. "I've been looking in Vienna."

"Looking at what?" Bruce asked.

"Not at. For."

"Looking for what?"

"My winnings."

"Your winnings?"

Gemma came in. She sniffed.

"You all right?" she asked. Bruce wanted her to stay but he was feeling muddled and could not think of a way to keep her there.

"Yes. I'm fine. You go on home," he said, going to the door with her to let her out.

"What's up?" she mouthed. Bruce shrugged, looking anxious. "I'll phone Mary," she indicated. Bruce gave a nod as Gemma left. He returned to Mandrake.

"What's up?" he asked, gingerly squeezing in so that he could crouch down beside him whilst somehow keeping a sliver of space between them. They were both hidden from view from the street.

"I've been to Vienna, right? To get my stuff from those bastard cheats, right? No chance. Nothing. Now they're after me." Mandrake broke off and crouched further behind the counter at the sound of feet running down the street.

Two men ran past. Bruce felt afraid. Did the act of running past his restaurant make them bad? But when he looked at Mandrake's face, the horror he saw there caused his own fear to surge. The sound of footsteps faded.

All was quiet. The fridges in the kitchen hummed and in the outhouse beyond, the washing machine worked on the day's linen. A couple of cars drove by in the fading light, the second one rattling slightly as it pulled by. The telephone rang. Mandrake grabbed at Bruce.

"No! Leave it!" Bruce was transfixed. The answer-phone cut in, inviting table bookings and the leaving of messages. Then Jenny spoke in her high, child's voice,

"Daddy, Mummy wants to know if you're going to be late. Are you there? I bet you can hear me. Are you coming? Myra and I have made you a pudding and Pascal has been in his room all day, not doing his homework. See you......What?" This was said to another person. The sound of talking away from the phone came through, then, "Mummy wants you to call back quickly." Jenny put down the telephone, deepening the silence in the room.

Suddenly, the two men who had run by earlier, returned. They were walking and running now, regaining their breath. They stopped at the restaurant and leaned against the plate window. Mandrake kept his grip on Bruce's arm, signalling with his face for absolute quiet and stillness.

Bruce could see nothing. He could only surmise by sound. He could hear the men talking in low voices, breathless at first. He could hear the rustle of their clothes and the taps and squeaks against the glass from what were probably the rivets in their jeans, or was it a knife or perhaps even a gun? Their feet shuffled. The silence and the fear held time suspended. Bruce felt electrified by it. His ears strained for information and could gather no more. His eyes took up the call and told him things of irrelevance.

He noticed for example, how the corner of a tray placed under the counter in a hasty moment, had a curious chip on it, shaped like a dog's head. It even had enough relief to throw a shadow to make an ear for it. Mandrake held himself as tense as an archer's string. 'Where's he going to shoot off to when released?' Bruce wondered.

Judging from the tone of their talking, the men reached agreement. They walked away. Bruce could hear them go. The tension and fear slipped. Mandrake released his grip. His brow was wet with the sweat of exertion and terror. Bruce's underarms itched ferociously as they always did after sudden fear or laughter.

"Right," said Mandrake. "Let's go."

"I have to phone Mary."

"Don't say nothing." Mandrake stood close to Bruce as he dialled. Bruce tried to turn away, but there he was again, breathing over him, foul breath, overlaid with sardine.

CHAPTER EIGHT

Some Kind Of Survival In Salzburg

By Salzburg Castle as evening fell, Zorcia lolled into the shadows of an ancient alcove. She could smell the musty stonework and feel its chill against her forehead as she drooped against it. The schnapps bottle in her pocket swung and knocked the wall, muffled by the lining of her coat. The sound of it both warmed and repelled her. Every drink was the same, a decision made in favour of oblivion and against her resolve. She drank deeply.

Daylight began to fade and starlings chattered incessantly as they gathered to roost. The hum of the traffic below drifted up the hillside and the trees in early leaf seemed to glow from within in response to the late sun. True to his routine of time and place, Zorcia's first client of the night arrived. He pulled aside her coat, hitched up her sweater, her skirt and took what he wanted. He held her to the wall with the weight of his body, leaning against her, his hands free to clutch and probe. He was quick, so quick that he never looked into her eyes or thought to hold her hand. Zorcia's heart gaped in pain as he filled her pockets with bottles and then left.

CHAPTER NINE

Bruce Rescued

For her birthday next week, Clive had decided to buy a bird table for Jenny. He had seen it in the pet shop window, displayed in the spring sale and he enjoyed the prospect of being able to give a special present that was within his budget.

Clive liked Jenny who always talked to him if they met at High Table. He made a point of remembering her birthday. He didn't have any children of his own because of the terrible mistake he had made with Zorcia. The mistake had broken his heart and filled him with shame and remorse. Why had he not had the guts to be strong for her? She occupied his thoughts often, yet how long ago it had all been. Sometimes, his dreams brought her so close that on waking, Clive struggled to accept that they had not really been together.

After such dreams, the joy of them lifted him for days. He had so nearly had her in his life all those years ago. The delight of that possibility, recreated in a dream, left him buoyant at first. Then, as daily life forced him to awaken yet again to his loss, he felt the agony of it all over again. Time did not seem to ease it at all. He had made a mistake and the consequences had left him with a disabled life.

He thought of Zorcia as he knew her then and of how she could be now if only they had stayed together. He could not achieve a picture of how she might be, at that moment. He could play around in his mind with any number of possibilities but fundamentally, he was certain that she was troubled.

Their first meeting had been in the mountains behind Split in what was then Yugoslavia. He had a day off from crewing on a private yacht and, setting off at first light, he had bought a whole day for solitude.

Taking a local bus, Clive chose a seat at the back, with its battered, blue leatherette. His thighs stuck to it in the heat which increased as the morning advanced, whilst the passengers crowded in for the journey to outlying villages. He hooked up his knees against the seat in front and leaned back to enjoy the view.

A man sat next to him, pulling a packet of cigarettes and a lighter from his worn, dark jacket. He nudged Clive who accepted the proffered smoke. The man lit up their cigarettes and they smoked together, nodding, smiling, reaching out.

As the bus began to climb the foothills, Clive watched the view changing from newly prospering town, to suburbs with their flower and vegetable patches. The further they went, so the spaces between houses grew, with goats, cows, orchards and farms spreading out before his eyes. The bus stopped at the request of the passengers, in villages, by houses and sometimes it seemed, in the middle of nowhere. When the man got off, he and Clive shook hands giving a final wave as the bus pulled away.

At the terminal village, well into the mountains, Clive walked swiftly through, only briefly acknowledging the curiosity of the villagers as he passed. He found a stream and followed it, walking through fields and woodland, hopping from rock to rock as he cut along the flood-bed, venturing higher still.

At midday, he rested below leafy trees, with nature in perfection. Sunlight sang all about him in tones of yellow and green. The stream uttered in joy as it fell across its bed. He lay down on the soft ground, his back cushioned by layers of grass and thyme. As he closed his lids, the sun made a sheen of silver in the tears that filled his lashes. Above him the leaves on the supple birches flicked and trembled, creating their own gentle sound, enriching the varied calls of the birds. Clive relished the lavish gifts of land that he had so desired whilst at sea.

In such a condition of pure delight, he became aware that he was not alone. He peeped. The movement of his lids made a tear escape. It ran down the side of his temple as he turned his head to see more clearly. Standing nearby was a girl as perfect as the day, Zorcia. They could not converse with words. They did not even attempt it. So, far from other people, they made a different choice, adding their simple love of life to the glowing day.

At first, as Zorcia sat down beside him, Clive, desiring her, had no expectation. They smiled together, both shy, both sensing their freedom. Clive shared his food with her, handing her bread, sausage, tomatoes and then, the whole of a prized Mars Bar. She ate with hunger and pleasure, repeatedly offering him back the partially finished chocolate which he refused. The delight on her face was feast enough for him.

After eating, they leaned back on their elbows, dipping their bare feet into the stream and feeling the warmth of the sun on the backs of their heads. As they dared to look deeply into each other's eyes, their unity was sealed. Time passed as the shadows from the trees dappled and moved around them.

Much later as evening approached, they made love, still sheltered by nature and her space. It was unique. It was extraordinary. It was beautiful. It was so unlikely to be believed that Clive had never told a soul. It was for them alone.

They had parted at dusk. There was so much love between them that there was no room for anything else. They accepted one another totally. Zorcia walked away, further up stream. Clive ran down to take the bus back to Split.

Now he was walking home with the bird table. He had picked it up after closing time. His friend Keith worked in the pet shop and they had arranged that Clive would go round to fetch the table at the end of the day and they would have a drink together. Clive reflected on their meeting - the tinned beers, some rather oily peanuts which had spilled out of their packet across the scratched, formica table and as usual, an emptiness between them which neither knew how to breach.

His way home would take him past High Table. It would be locked up by now. It was a good place to go. With so many other people around, his loneliness was soaked up. There was always a way to join in.

As he approached the restaurant, Clive paused to scrutinize the bargains in the travel agent's window. The street was deserted. Then he heard a door opening and looking up, he saw a strange man come furtively out of High Table. After a glance up and down the street, he briefly disappeared before emerging with Bruce. He was holding Bruce's arm and Bruce was leaning away from the man. They had not seen him standing in the shop doorway. Clive stepped back further into the recess as they walked towards him with Bruce on the inside.

Quietly, Clive put down the bird table. The pale price label flickered in the light breeze. He held it still to keep the movement from attracting attention.

A passing car threw light onto the stranger's face. Clive knew him. It was the notorious Mandrake looking even wilder and more hunted than usual. Their paths had crossed often at the hospital. Bruce looked grim and pale and his eyes were dark with emotion. He needed help. As they passed the doorway, Clive stepped out, pushing Mandrake off the pavement. He took Bruce's arm.

"Run!" Clive shouted. Bruce sprang into life. They ran. A screech of brakes behind them caused them to look back over their shoulders. A shiny, dark car with black windows had stopped at an angle to the pavement. They were just in time to see the door slam as it slewed away. Mandrake was nowhere to be seen.

CHAPTER TEN

War Begins Within

Mary felt utterly drained of all her sweetness. After a morning of wounding frustration she had kept going on tension, acting out the part that she ascribed herself. Pascal had bitterly remained in his room, remote at lunch time and quiet upstairs for the rest of the day. She felt hollowed out by confusion.

Jenny and Myra had spent the rest of the day cooking and then watching television. Mary thought television a waste of a friend's visit, but chose not to take on any more. She had declined to play with them after all. She had buried herself in the ironing, thereby suggesting that it was essential and came before playing with her own daughter. She was then able to imply that she would rather play, but not when she had so much that she must do. A question tugged unkindly at her all afternoon, 'Is this your best?' and she supposed that it was. Mary longed for Bruce to come home, bringing change with him.

First, a knock at the door brought Myra's mother. They had not met before. She declined an offer of tea and hovered just inside the door. The girls came down, Myra bringing shoes in her wake, sitting on the bottom stair to put them on.

"Hurry Myra," urged her mother. "You have your piano lesson to fit in before gym club." She looked at Mary. "I don't believe in can't. Children today have so many opportunities and I want Myra to take as many as I can manage for her." This was said with triumph and authority. Mary felt put down. She did not hear the defensive element in the voice. "What with working all day," here she paused, looking about at a home in disarray, "I have to be very organised and that's the way I want it. That's the way I have to be. I have got the sort of mind that would seize up if I was just at home all day."

Jenny and Myra went quiet, each trying to understand this interaction between adults and where it fitted into the requirements of good manners. They noticed that both women were flushed. They looked at each other and flushed too. Myra thanked Mary for her day and left with her mother.

"How was your day?" Mary asked Jenny as she wondered to herself why people spoke to her as Myra's mother had.

"All right," she said.

Still no Bruce. Mary was counting on him to break the stale-mate between her and Pascal, to praise and enjoy Jenny's pudding, to listen to her heavy troubles, to simply be present and bring in his steadiness. Everything in the house ached for his return. The telephone rang.

"Mary? It's Gemma." Mary liked Gemma. Just now her friendly, husky voice, in contrast to the strident tones of Myra's mother, filled her with pleasure, longing and relief all at once. She could hear Gemma smoking.

"Hullo Gemma. How are you? Do you want Bruce? He's not back yet. He's late."

"That's why I'm ringing. Mandrake's in High Table. He sort of barged in just as we were shutting. Bruce didn't look too happy so I said I'd give you a bell. I don't know what it's all about, but I said I'd call, so I'm calling."

"Thanks Gemma. That's very out of the blue. We haven't seen Mandrake since we moved here. What did he want?"

"All I can say is that Mandrake was giving off mighty bad vibes. He looked a mess, not that that's anything unusual, but a mess even for Mandrake, I mean. Bruce was giving him the left-overs to eat."

"Do you think I should go round?"

"I've only just left, really. He's probably still there. You could ring him, try and catch him."

43

"Yes. Yes, I'll try that then. Thanks Gemma." They put down their receivers.

Feeling uneasy, Mary drifted back to the kitchen and began to prepare supper. After scrabbling in the potato sack and picking them out into a colander, she began to peel one before grinding to a halt as its coat of dry earth turned to mud beneath the tap. She was aware of the increasing coldness of the water and, hence, her hand. The potato became slippery and she responded by tightening her grip, preoccupied by the feeling that she was on the brink of drama.

Mary just wanted everything to be still and simple. In this longing for quiet, she kept as still as she could, trying to stop the movement of her life. There was nothing before her but great, shadowy hurdles. She could see no way to live without having to surmount them. If she could just keep still she would not have to jump, although it seemed that the more she tried to remain static, the closer the hurdles came to her. She had worked so hard to make everything right, but what she had achieved felt no better than a paralysis of fear.

Jenny came in, bringing a question that pulled Mary from her unhappy trance.

"Where's Daddy?"

"You can phone him. Tell him about your pudding." She heard Jenny speaking to the answer phone. Her fingers ached with cold. She turned off the tap and ran some warm water into a bowl. "Tell him to call back soon," she called out.

"What?"

"Tell him to call back quickly!" If he didn't, what would she do? If he was in the restaurant, why did he not cut in when he heard Jenny's voice? He always did. Perhaps Mandrake had left and Bruce was now on his way home. But then, if he knew that Gemma was phoning, he would surely ring to reassure her. Mary's unease increased.

Time passed but indecision did not. Then the telephone rang and Jenny answered it. Mary could hear her talking.

"You don't need Mummy. She's cooking. I can take a message." A pause followed. "Why can't I tell her? Tell me and I'll tell her." Mary took the phone and Jenny, hurt and puzzled, went to sit on the bottom stair in the hall.

"Bruce?"

"Mary!" His voice was strained. "I'm going to be late home." The line went dead, leaving Mary holding the receiver, feeling fear for Bruce, for all of them, pricking at the inside of her skin.

"Jenny! Shut the dogs in the kitchen. We're going to fetch Daddy." Sensing her mother's urgency, Jenny obeyed without hesitation. Mary went upstairs to fetch Pascal. He was sitting at his desk, deeply engrossed by an unravelled paper-clip as a perfect tool for boring into a rubber. He wore only shorts and a tee shirt. She gathered a jersey, socks and shoes and began to dress him. "We're in a hurry. Daddy wants us to fetch him quickly. You'd better leave all this for now." Pascal held out his feet, pushing them into each presented sock. He kept hold of the paper-clip. He had folded it back on itself and was threading it into the fabric of his jersey. His foot went floppy as his attention refocused.

"Wake up Pascal and help me!" Mary shouted.

CHAPTER ELEVEN
Bruce Comes Home

Mary started the engine of the car and began to pull out of the drive. Then she remembered that she had not got the restaurant keys.

"Where are you going now?" the children asked, imitating the tone of exasperation that she might use in the midst of their muddling.

"Keys!", she called back softly, bending back into the car. "Hush now." She ran inside to be welcomed by the dogs, ecstatic at her return before resigning themselves back to their beds in recognition of this familiar, second abandonment. Grabbing the keys, she ran back to the car. She felt alive with purpose.

Mary drove gently, tending to the car, its gears and its switches with a soft touch. All about her and with her, felt precious. She wanted her every move to count.

The lanes were quiet as they made their way, filling with traffic as they approached the city. The children sat silently in the back of the car. Pascal watched his breath condense and fade, condense and fade upon the window. He was out of his room, anything was better than being in there, facing defeat without hope. Jenny looked at the back of her mother's head. She could smell her perfume and felt the need for a hug. She extended her shoeless leg and put her foot gently on Mary's shoulder. Mary put her hand to it between tending to the driving.

"What's happened Mummy?" she asked. "Has Daddy broken down?"

"I don't know if anything much has happened. I just felt that we should go and see if Daddy needs us. I'm not really sure if he's at High Table. He may be on his way home. Just keep an eye open for his car in case you can spot him." They were driving through a run-down shopping centre, lit by the orange glow of street lamps.

"There he is! He's walking with Clive!" cried Jenny. Mary slowed the car and joined Pascal in the search. The light was dim and disorientating, but as Bruce and Clive stepped out of the shadows, she saw them too.

"I can see them!" called Pascal, as Mary looped the car round. The men ran to her. Clive got into the front and Bruce flopped into the back, embracing his children silently.

"Thank God! Let's go home," he said.

No one spoke. It was a waiting time. As they travelled, Bruce sank into this comfort whilst Clive sat leaning forward, alert. They pulled slowly into the drive. The front door was wide open and they could hear the dogs barking in the kitchen.

"Get this car back out of the drive fast!" urged Clive. "Turn off your lights. Whoever is there may not have heard us because of the dogs." Mary reversed back, swinging neatly round the corner and into the road.

"Now what?" she asked as she put up her hand to turn off the engine.

"No, wait!" Clive restrained her hand. She looked at him. "Just keep it running in case we need to move fast." He turned to Bruce. "Wake up Bruce!" Bruce jerked out of his torpor and began to pay attention. "Mary, we're getting out. Take the children away from here."

The two men began to get out of the car. As Bruce crept past Jenny, she grabbed his sleeve and tried to pull him back. Bruce was frightened, intent on getting away from his family and preparing to protect them. He jerked his arm away from her and continued to squeeze by.

"Daddy!" she whispered.

"No Jenny!" he hissed.

"I think the front door has just blown open. I don't think it got shut properly when Myra went."

"What's that?" Mary said, in a cross, panicking voice, alarmed that this strange turn of events could have been caused by her negligence. At the same time, she realised that Jenny was right, recalling that she had not dropped the latch as Myra and her mother left and they themselves had gone out through the back door. "I think Jenny is right."

Bruce sat back down. Clive nodded to Mary and she pulled the car forward. The built up tension eased as she drove back through the gateway. Nothing had changed in the few moments that had passed, except that Roger was now howling.

In the house all was as it had been left. The dogs hurled themselves at the family before racing out into the garden. The potatoes remained unpeeled in the sink. Mary jostled them as she made room to fill the kettle.

"Look at my pudding Daddy," said Jenny. Mary turned to enjoy Bruce's response, but his face was crowded with shadows. His head hung over the offered dish and he could not see what was there. Jenny looked up at her father. The way his eyes looked but did not see made her sad and frightened. Pascal came over and looked at the pudding.

"I made one like that once," he said.

When Clive came in he touched Jenny lightly on her shoulder and then turned to Bruce. Bruce looked at him, his face full of need as he put out his arms to be held. Clive took him, held him still.

Mary, Pascal and Jenny watched this in silence, unknowing. The kettle began to murmur, boiled and then clicked off, but no one moved. The need for tea was irrelevant in the midst of this. For each of them, the Bruce that they needed had not come home.

Gradually, Bruce was able to let go of Clive. Mary began to make tea. The children cautiously approached their father and stood by him. Clive lit a cigarette.

"What's going on?" Mary asked.

"Bruce?" Clive invited.

"I don't know," he said in a baffled, quaking voice. "Nothing much when you put it into words. I mean, Mandrake is always disturbing, isn't he? And marching into High Table like that was odd, but no more. But he was terrified, that's the point and he was using me as some kind of shield. Then Clive appeared from nowhere and then Mandrake disappeared. He's been taken away. By who? Why? I feel like I've been snatched into another, horrible dimension and I want to get back into my life without this taint and without this feeling of us all being in danger, or of having to think about the people who live like that all the time."

Mary could feel her own fear rising in response to what Bruce said. What could she do now to save them all from the world?

CHAPTER TWELVE

Mandrake Loses Out

In the back of the car, Mandrake lay on the floor. He had expected to be caught so that despite his fear, the situation seemed strangely natural. He need no longer dread and run, but now he was helpless.

Mandrake had been forced to the floor and was pinned against the back of the front seats by the feet of a man. If he moved the man kicked him, so he kept still and tried to think, but all that he could think about was how he wanted to pee, how he wanted to fight the man, how he needed to breathe more, but most of all, increasingly, overbearingly, he wanted to know from where, or how he would get his next fix.

The man had his feet hard against his ribs. He could only breathe shallowly and the air was thick and dusty. He had been punched and winded when they pulled him into the car. He did not know how long he had been like this. He had lost track of time, but judging by his bladder, they had covered many miles.

"I got to piss," he said, but the feet jabbed at him.

"You'll do," came the reply and Mandrake had to stay.

As the car sped on, he began to slip in his mind. He thought of his home, Stonelea and its loss. He thought of Vienna. He thought of his mother whom he could hardly remember and of his grandmother. How he longed for her to comfort him again. His head spun down there, pinned to the gritty floor.

Mandrake had been born of a gypsy family at a time when their way of life was being dramatically affected by changing by-laws and post war housing policies. His name then was Robin. His first years were lived in the close community of his extended family until shortly before his sister was born.

His mother, father and he were given a council house to live in and although none of them wanted this at the time, it had become increasingly difficult to resist. His parents Colin and Sheila were very young, inexperienced and unformed. They had been confused by the authority of other people - the landowners, schools, health workers and police.

The Birch's new house was well outside a village which was itself rural and remote. Inside it were the things that go with houses - a cooker, electricity, a fence around the garden, and these things were not the Birch's way. After Robin burned his hand on the cooker hob, Sheila took to cooking on a fire again. Her son knew of the danger from the red-hot sticks and ashes.

At first they gleaned fuel from the nearby woods, but after being seen off by the landowner, Slater, they broke down the fence for fuel. They had no money to buy more. There was not enough work locally of the sort that Colin could do. Besides, there was little trust from neighbours who feared them because they would not be moving on.

Locals took this fence removal as evidence that, as popular myth decreed, gypsies were indeed unsociable. The Birch family was shunned. Robin, having begun life surrounded by welcoming people and an abundance of related playmates, now had no friends. His sister when she was born, filled him with pride, but she was not yet a companion.

His parents muddled on. Colin drank and it was often too much. These times were not forgotten by the villagers; the times when he shouted across the intimate groupings in the pub, speaking broadly and incomprehensibly, disturbing people. He never hurt anyone. He never directly threatened. His shouting was about his own faults, a keening lament for his inability to discover how to join in, clothed in questions about village life. No one wanted to listen to such distress. They thought he might be going to blame them.

They had given him a house and it hadn't sorted things out. Instead, it caused this unhappy man to linger in their community, displaying his entrapment and his loss of liberty and purpose. It threw uncomfortable questions into the air around them and there they hung. Colin represented the unsolved or worse still, his very presence hinted at the unsolvable. People turned away from the challenge that he and his family unwittingly posed.

Yet a man like Slater, after drink and often without it, humiliated his children and his wife. He teased his dogs and beat them if he deemed them to be disobedient in their confusion. He sacked and evicted people from their jobs and homes, keeping his charm for those he chose. He hurt people and animals and yet was tolerated, invited to parties, greeted in the village. Colin had observed this, but making any sense of it was impossible.

Robin spent much time alone in those early years. He watched, snatching pieces of jigsaw to try to fit into his puzzle picture of life. He knew his father's value, recalling the days when he had been fit and busy, helping to make things and events work. Now, and it had something to do with the glaring removal of the fence for firewood, he was despised, his mother patronised and excluded.

To get to school Robin was left to do the lonely walk as other children were teamed up by their parents and taken in cars. Sometimes he was offered a lift, but he always refused. He sensed that it would gratify them to help him so he withheld their chances. They only did it when it suited them to offer the seat left vacant by a briefly sick child. He chose to walk.

His sister Mandy was ill. If she had been going to school in a car, there would have been a vacant seat often. Her chest was weak because of the cold and damp. Heating the house was expensive. There were no fire placcs. The house was powered solely by electricity. The family lurched between debt, being cut off and being helped by the social worker. In the weeks that passed as the damp and cold built up, unabated by warmth, Mandy suffered. So did the next baby, Steven, who died at four months leaving Sheila frail with sorrow.

At Steven's death, Sheila could go no further. She was suspended in despair and could not conceive an exit. Her mother came to live with them. Gwendolyne too suffered from this loss, yet she was able to keep strength for her grieving daughter and family. She could interpret the house, its needs and how to meet them. Gwendolyne brought this strength right into the heart of the family and each of them responded in time. For her, it brought its own healing and spared her the frozen loneliness which had begun to prowl at the edges of her life the moment, three years before, when she had been widowed.

Mandy thrived as the warmth of loving order spread. Neighbours, shocked and somehow shamed by the death of a baby, brought clothes, logs and food in small, shy amounts. Gwendolyne, sure of herself, gave thanks. People were encouraged and brought more.

Although Robin continued to walk to school, he now had a mackintosh and wellington boots. Sheila sat in the kitchen, pinched only by her loss and not the cold. Sometimes she smiled to herself and then she began to smile at others, yet she remained passive.

With his mother-in-law to steady them, Colin stayed at home more and began to put the house right. He made a shelf in Robin's room. Onto this, Robin put his best things, acquired through his own means. There was the marble that he had won in the playground; an ammonite; a dried, bright red leaf and a stone with a rim of tiny crystals along one, short edge. There was a small, toy lorry that he had kept after it had been thrown at him over a hedge by children playing together in the village. He had responded by lobbing a dried-out dog turd back at them, causing hysterical screams and even tears. Robin put the lorry in his pocket and took it home. If they could spare it to throw, they didn't need it. It wasn't stealing.

CHAPTER THIRTEEN

Death of a Life

It became known in the village, quietly as water soaking into a sponge, that Gwendolyne had wisdom. She would listen to problems and help to find solutions. This was her way of giving something in return. The house once so empty of homely cohesion, now held all that was needed to bring it to life. Whilst remaining bare of many comforts, it now contained the business of people who came, talked and shared.

There was a table with odd chairs in the kitchen. Colin had painted them pale blue, so they did match after all. There was tea in a jar. There were broken biscuits, tumbled in a cream coloured Coronation tin, the Queen's face and her coat of arms worn away by the chips and scratches of daily use. Children played on the floor, sharing a mix of marbles, bricks, a metal crane and an old bakelite doll wearing home knitted clothes. It became a place of welcome.

Robin continued to watch. He was quiet. Those who came were too much in awe of Gwendolyne to express their diffidence at the presence of her grandson and she never asked him to leave. Robin was captivated by the concentration of the women as they offered themselves to Gwendolyne, seeking knowledge. She invited questions, never balking at what needed to be heard or spoken.

Women asked about their children, their husbands, health and money. They asked about love, temptation, deceit and lust. Some wanted to hurt and punish, some to forgive. Some wanted to manipulate their worlds, some to escape. Others desired truth and purpose.

Slater's daughter Lucy came with her friend, Marianne. Both in their teens, they were shy and flustered - Lucy the more so. As Gwendolyne answered their tentative knock on the door, they hesitated before stepping over the threshold, into her kitchen, into her world.

As soon as the door was shut behind them, Lucy burst into tears, turning away from her friend and from Gwendolyne in her agony. Marianne tried to explain their presence.

"I'm Marianne and this is my friend Lucy and..."

"I know who you are," Gwendolyne replied. "You are welcome to this home." She walked over to the table, pulled out the chairs and gently signalled to Marianne who brought Lucy over and sat her down. Robin was lying on a mat by the fire, staring into the multiple coils of wire that encircled the electric element. He could feel the skin tighten on his face in the glowing heat. He watched the girls as they settled at the table. Robin thought them very pretty and to him, they seemed grown up, yet when they sat beside his grandmother, they looked more like children. Lucy began to cry again. Marianne put her arm around her. After a few moments Gwendolyne said,

"Leave her now Marianne. Take your arm away and let Lucy find herself now." Marianne felt criticised and her hurt showed. "I know you want to help her, dear, so sit beside her quietly and let her have her say. If you stay like that she won't have the room she needs to find her own way. She'll be too busy trying to oblige you by cheering up, whether or not she's ready. Do you see?" Marianne nodded and pulled her arm away, close to tears herself.

'She's learning too,' Robin observed to himself. Lucy cried on. She was afraid of everything that came into her head; her problem, its history, the way there was something wrong with any solution she could muster. She was frightened to give voice to the thoughts that jostled in her head.

Gwendolyne recognised this and understood it. She had witnessed so many people caught up in such fear and knew that all of them stood on the threshold of an awakening. For some, this opportunity would be crushed, the occasion seeming to challenge them more than they felt able to handle. Some might be overwhelmed and drift or freeze whilst events took over. For others though, it brought a time to leap forward and spring out of constraints suddenly revealed as paper tigers, bringing liberation and renewal. What would Lucy choose?

"Now, ducky," said Gwendolyne, "it's time. Tell me about it." Lucy tried to talk. She had been crying so much during the last few hours that she was exhausted, her thoughts riding on waves of emotion and confusion.

"I don't know, I don't know!" she cried. "I don't know what to do. Mummy's gone. Daddy's finally driven her away. I hate him! I hate him!" The words came out, jarred by Lucy's sobs, her gulps for air and vain attempts to compose herself.

"Last night, she was going to go out, but Daddy didn't want her to so he locked her in the house. He locked me in too and just shouted and shouted. I thought Mummy was going to be ill again."

This recollection brought Lucy's fear back afresh. Her voice became unpredictable, wobbling as she tried to stop herself from crying again. She sniffed, trying to find a hanky up her sleeve to mop up the mess that comes with distress, emphasising our neediness. There was no hanky and Lucy's dripping nose stopped her thoughts. No one had a handkerchief and in those days of Bronco toilet paper, before kitchen towels and boxes of tissues became standard in homes, Lucy sniffed again as she tried to collect herself.

"Daddy just shouted all over the place, so I took the key anyway and Mummy got out. She hasn't come back yet and the thing is," Lucy hesitated, weighing up how to tell and if to tell. She looked at Gwendolyne who met her eyes steadily and with acceptance. Lucy sighed shakily. "The thing is, I'm not staying in the house without her. I just can't. It's... it's not...I mean, without Mummy, Daddy..." Lucy suddenly tensed and a rush of blood swept to her face. She stumbled for words. For the second time, Gwendolyne caught her eyes, conveying the understanding that Lucy craved. Marianne missed this moment. She was poking the sugar in the bowl, making little heaps, patting them down with the spoon and then reforming them. The quiet caused her to stop and look up. Robin knew that without words, something had been given, but he didn't know what.

"I know," said Gwendolyne. She waited as Lucy's tension eased.

"He's a bully. I'm frightened." This last word was wailed with renewed misery as feelings of hopelessness returned to swamp her.

A car stopped suddenly outside the house. Leaving the engine running, the driver slammed the car door and lumbered towards the house. They all turned as he passed the window. Lucy drew back as the sudden bang of her father's body-weight thudded against the front door. He wrenched it open and almost fell into the kitchen. He was drunk with whisky and the fury with which he defended himself from self-loathing.

Lucy leapt up to shelter behind Gwendolyne, clutching at Marianne who joined her there. Robin stayed still. Gwendolyne stood up slowly in order to face Slater with calm. He thrust himself at her, raising his fist as his face darkened with threats.

"Gerald!" she said, quickly, sharply. He paused. She took his hand and held it in both of hers. When he looked at her, he saw that he was safe. She did not judge him. Momentarily, he experienced profound relief, a sense that he truly could let go of his burden that demanded so much from him. He paused, but then pride swept at him again, overturning that briefly gifted vision of peace. He lunged forward, catching Gwendolyne catastrophically, punching her breastbone with his free hand. She staggered backwards and, as the two girls tried in vain to catch her, began to slump beyond their strength to support her. Robin ran to her. To those there, it all seemed to be happening in slow motion, although in fact, things were happening so fast that no one could prevent Gwendolyne from falling and striking her head on a corner of the table as she collapsed.

After a lifetime of storming the boundaries of decency and of ignoring the consequences of his actions, Slater now struck the granite face of truth with shattering speed. He was a killer, hot blooded and wrong. Children stared at him from all sides. Robin had wet himself. In the centre of Gwendolyne's brow, a dark bruise surrounded a small ooze of blood.

Mandrake could not think about that time without reawakening the fear and grief. In years it measured quite a distance, but in resolution, time had stood still. In all that had happened to him since, he had not found a way to stop the pain. All his attempts had only made the wounds more raw.

The man began to kick him and to complain.

"You stink! You heap of shit! Open the window Vic. He's pissed himself!" The night air swept along Mandrake's body. He was cold. He was wet. Nausea took him. He was without influence, alone again and beginning to suffer withdrawal.

CHAPTER FOURTEEN

Holding Tight But Slipping

Zorcia could not often remember what she wanted. There were things she had to do, but her focus would slip. There was nothing in her life that she wanted to see or to dwell upon. Sometime long ago, life had not been the threadbare rag of existence that she now endured. It had once been glorious. That glory was now shrouded by the present.

She had a room in a basement, next to an ancient bakery. The cracked stone steps leading down to her shared entrance were uneven with weeds. Rye dust was layered on every surface, blotting the colours, dull though they were, and diminishing her image in the dark panes of her windows. They reflected her as she stole about her room, a ghost with ennui.

This desperate life, parched with loneliness, forced into movement only by the clamour of her body for food and shelter, was relentlessly unrewarding. She was shunned by the baking community and had only awkward encounters with those who shared her door. Early hopes of red geraniums for the summer had died beneath the relentless dust which, after a fall of rain, formed into glue and sealed off the soil in her window box.

Isolated by the constraints of illegal immigration, Zorcia struggled through her daily escape from death. For a while she had maintained her hope in life with intelligence, but now she kept that part of herself confined to a shining place just outside of her head, slightly to the left and above. This was where she contained and tethered her memories of a beautiful life. This would be her route to redemption. For the rest of herself she was simply muddling through until the time could come to reel in her shining ball and she would begin to feel and live again.

She had been born into wholeness, without a need to protect or cut off any part of herself from life. She grew up glowing with joy in the abundant life around her. The community of her village was a life-form and the plants, both wild and cultivated, were part of it. When she climbed a tree or great rocks, she could feel their pulse beneath her hands and feet. As they shimmered with life, so did she. The day that she took the English sailor for her lover, she was simply doing what she had done all her life.

When Clive had left at the end of that day of beauty, she felt no wrench, just more love. It was a natural recognition of the freedom that all of life requires in order to be able to express its unity. Her loving heart bore no wound on account of his departure.

CHAPTER FIFTEEN

Ignorant Visitors

Some months after Clive, a small group of five English students came to Zorcia's village. They had no perception of their impact and came with a shallow desire for adventure and traveller's tales to take back to the student bars in the autumn.

They were making their journey in a battered van, parking in lay-bys, washing in mountain streams with shampoo and detergent, taking vegetables from farms and gardens, believing themselves to be getting back to nature. They were naïve and careless of the world. They talked a great deal and considered themselves to be very deep, perhaps even revolutionary, thinkers. They discussed whether or not it was possible to have absolute historical truth and the tragedy of war, whilst having no awareness of the impact of their own thoughts and behaviour. Self-righteously, they complained to one another of the assorted pollutions that they witnessed on their journey. It never occurred to them to examine their own levels of toxicity.

So in this way, they came upon Zorcia's village. They arrived at night, driving the van onto what seemed like a small open field cropped by sheep. They enjoyed their pride at sleeping beneath the stars so many miles from home.

In the morning they were awakened by the quiet voices of the villagers who for some time had been pacing around their sleeping forms. The students had miscalculated their campsite and parked close to a group of houses. As Mick opened his eyes, they met with curiosity above him, expressed by peering eyes, heads turned a little to the side and mouths dropped open.

Mick turned to the others, their grubby sleeping bags lying at angles to each other like fallen maggots. Despite a sense of pleasure at being the centre of attention, he could not prevent a streak of shame from flitting through his mind. He smiled weakly at the on-lookers and blushed, feeling unable to get out of his bag. He had on only underpants, his jeans and tee-shirt being rolled to make a pillow. His awkwardness increased.

When Mick called to the others, the villagers began to talk amongst themselves, their voices rising to normal levels. John and Pete stirred. The voices rose a little further. When Liz and Sue awoke, raising their faces from the mouths of their bags, a tension came and a woman began to shout at them.

"We can't get up in front of everybody," Liz said desperately.

"Let's do a sort of sack race thing to the van and get out of here," said Pete. All five of them struggled to get up. Sue tried to get their audience to laugh, but her attempts at eye contact brought further anger. Before they could all get to the van, a group of boys had opened the back and were examining the jumble of possessions lying there. One had unearthed their torch and was playing with it, flicking it on and off, making the red flasher go. Liz felt outrage at their invasion. She saw no parallel in her own behaviour. She snatched the torch and threw it into the back before heaving herself in.

John had the ignition keys. He scrambled into the driver's seat, pulling off his sleeping bag as he did so. He started the engine, pulling away as Mick threw himself into the back, the doors alternately banging and wrenching at their hinges.

As they pulled away, a police car drove up with headlights and siren blaring. It blocked their escape and forced them to stop. Everyone tried to put on their clothes, although Pete only had time to drape a towel over his lap. A policeman came up to his window.

"Go!" he said. "Not here tourists. Go! Big road only!" and with his fist, he thumped all along the side of the van as they pulled away. The friends were subdued. Sue was frightened, as were they all, but only she cried. It was the shock of hitting a separate reality and being thrown out of it. They went on to continue their holiday. Behind, in Zorcia's village, an old soup packet, a sandal and three turds lay on the grass.

CHAPTER SIXTEEN

Keeping The Battens Down With Polite Performance

"All I can say," said Bruce, "is that he would have harmed me. I felt so helpless. I could think of no way out. If Clive had not come...", his voice trailed away. Mary took his mug and poured more tea. When she gave it back, she took his cold hand and with her own, she folded it round the warmth of the mug.

"That's bad enough," she said, "but why all the creeping in stuff when we got home? Why such a response to the open door? Were you just jumpy after what happened, or is there something else to tell?"

"There is more," said Clive, "but we're not sure what. We've hardly had time to talk, let alone think and be able to make sense of anything. Apart from not knowing where Mandrake was heading, it's something that he said that has shaken us up. Tell them Bruce."

"Wait," said Mary, "let's talk later." As Bruce and Clive had begun to talk, Jenny had crept onto her lap, cuddling into her and holding the edge of her jersey as she always did when she became anxious. Pascal was giving his full attention and his eyes had widened in early alarm. "Let's eat. We're all hungry, especially the children," she added a little pointedly.

"Yes. We'll eat," Bruce agreed. "What have we got?"

"There's my pudding!" Jenny reminded them all.

"And what could make a Saturday evening better than the chance of a delicious pudding, made by one of my favourite people?" said Clive.

"Yes, and let's have those bread rolls and whatever we can find in the fridge," said Mary, putting cheeses, paté and tomatoes on to the table. "Pascal, can you do the mats and plates, please?"

They sat around the table. A rush of hunger quietened them as they passed around food and ate. Then Jenny got up to fetch her pudding, just as the telephone rang. She danced out to answer it.

"Leave it!" called Mary, but it was too late. Jenny returned.

"It's for you Mummy. It's Mr Croft. What does he want?" she asked.

"I don't know," she answered as she went to take the call. She had been trying to get hold of Pascal's head teacher for most of the term. Now of all times, he had rung. She thought of all the occasions when she had been put off by the school, when Mr Croft's business had superseded any notion of other people's business. She could even claim that she had been feeling desperate to talk to him and on another evening she would have felt triumphant that he was calling her. But now? She could not afford to put him off, yet at the same time, she wanted to support Bruce and to stop him and Clive from frightening the children further. Once more, she felt the strain of conflicting interests wearing her down.

"Hullo? Mr Croft? It's Mrs Mosaic."

"Ah yes. My secretary tells me that you have been wanting to speak to me. I don't usually contact parents at the weekend. However as it sounded urgent and I got caught up yesterday afternoon when I had hoped to ring you, I thought that I would make a special effort and call you now." His voice was deep, with a preened charm that was clearly superficial to the discerning. The favour he believed himself to be doing, oozed complacently from every word he spoke. "What is it that you want to talk about?"

Mary was grateful for this contact, but she felt uncomfortable too - patronised and aware of Mr Croft's disregard of the value of her own time. Resentment thundered low in her stomach at the way he assumed the power to listen, or not.

"It's Pascal," she began.

"Ah, Pascal," replied Mr Croft with resignation.

"Things are still not right," said Mary, regretting the way her voice moved up several pitches. She anxiously noted how this sounded more like an accusation than an observation for reasoned consideration. She could feel Mr Croft switching off. What could she say that he would hear? She sighed. "Mr Croft, Pascal's still not wanting to go to school. He won't do his homework. There is always a fuss. He's unhappy."

"Mrs Mosaic, we have discussed this before." Croft sounded as if he was spelling out a word that she should already know how to write. "I see Pascal every day and I can assure you that he is perfectly all right at school. Are there any difficulties at home perhaps?"

Mary pictured Mr Croft in his home. He lived in a new bungalow which was suffocatingly neat on the outside. If he was sitting, his large belly would be resting on his thighs, forcing them apart in order to be accommodated. He was probably wearing grey, a jersey perhaps, with pink and cream diamonds knitted into it. Not enough pattern to disguise his diminutive chest with its unmanly, breast-like fat.

His fat was not benevolent or jolly, like a Buddha or Mr Pickwick. It was an oily defence. It had probably come into being, cell by cell, each time he had refused to listen when it had been his job to do so. He had encased himself in deafening fat, built on denial. To suggest that Pascal's trouble came solely from his home perfectly demonstrated the effectiveness of this fat.

Through the door, Mary could hear the others. Pascal was talking with animation and intelligence, making the others laugh.

"No," she said. "Everything's fine here. There's nothing to upset him. He's cheerful and interested in everything. It's always the school things."

"Well you see, Mrs Mosaic, some children take longer than others to settle in. They can't all mature at the same rate." He paused as if to emphasize his use of the word mature. "I'll talk to Mrs Windspill. She is his teacher, isn't she? I'll ask her to keep an eye on him. You leave it to us professionals and don't allow him to know how anxious you are. It never helps children if they think that they can play on their parents' worries."

In this pause, Mary could see his chins wobbling in assurance of the right knowledge to which they were a party, being so closely hung beneath the very mouth that was imparting such unquestionable jewels of wisdom.

"I am sure that there is nothing of any great import here. Pascal will get the hang of co-operating with school life before long."

Mr Croft awaited thanks, but Mary was speechless. She floated into her emergency survival gear and pretended to be who she was not.

"Thank you Mr Croft. Thank you for sparing the time," her voice said.

"Well, if that'll be all then, goodbye." Croft put down the phone swiftly.

"Goodbye," Mary said to the air as she replaced the receiver. Her emotions churned within and around her and she could not settle them. Mr Croft had offered nothing of any use. He had made no attempt to get to the root of the matter. His talking to Mrs Windspill would be unlikely to change anything for Pascal, yet it would almost certainly reduce her credibility even further.

The last thing that she wanted was to be a fussy or interfering mother. To her, Pascal was a distressed child, genuinely unhappy and at odds with his schooling. Other children seemed to be coping with it all, joining in, having fun and making friends. Whenever she tried to confide her concerns to other mothers, she was swiftly met with a proud account of how well their children were doing. It was now almost too painful to confide in anyone. She had used up her listening ears anyway.

Mary was deeply aware that Pascal was in trouble, but no one else could see it and she was beginning to believe the line they spun her.

"You are over anxious and this is the cause of his lack of confidence. Back off and give him the space to be himself. Your pride in him is misplaced. He is not as bright as you think. You are expecting too much from him."

Back in the kitchen, Jenny had kept everyone at bay, her pudding waiting unbroken on the table.

"Now, time for my pudding every one," she said, as Mary rejoined them. Jenny had decorated the top with hundreds and thousands, silver balls and chocolate strands. It was much admired and then eaten. Afterwards, Mary took the children to bed.

Each child needed help, reminders, nudges and then a story. All the time, a pulse of fearfulness ran through Mary's body. She acted out the part she wished to be, that of loving mother at bed time, although throughout, her mind dwelt on the telephone call with Mr Croft. Her sense of personal foolishness mingled with frustration and her desire to talk to Bruce and Clive. This was a remarkable skill, to be able to read aloud from a book with animation and yet to be quite elsewhere.

CHAPTER SEVENTEEN

Mandrake Dismissed

Mandrake lay incapacitated by his own hell of withdrawal. His captors paid no regard to his needs and had no understanding of his danger. They wanted information from him but could get nothing from this insensible man. They did not view him with compassion, but as a malfunctioning tool.

He was lying on the concrete floor of an empty warehouse which was littered with dirty, brittle plastic wrapping and layered with rusty flakes of metal. Chilling night air, coursing in through high broken windows, sank into the building, spreading damp. In the distance traffic droned, interrupted only by the sound of passing night trains which clattered by with erratic rhythm, shaking more dust from the roof and walls. Streaks of lamplight edged into this great space from the outside, casting black shadows.

Mandrake looked up from the floor but he could not focus on anything. Sweat poured from him and he shivered wildly. He saw dark shapes around him. Were they moving? They might be spinning or he might be spinning, he couldn't tell. He was too distracted. Sharp pains pierced his joints before shooting out like red-hot wires to be transmitted along his limbs, round his throat and his chest to tighten, tug and ensnare.

Mandrake held up his forearm into a beam of light. It was bright orange, bulging with dark scarlet spots which writhed into lines and back again. He moved his arm, in and out of the beam, flickering, light and dark, light and dark. In his hallucination Slater's face lurched from a graze on his wrist bone, his mouth sealed over, his lips trying to pull apart but held by a purple, stranded membrane. The membrane burst, Slater's face becoming like an anus, peeling away from the emerging gulls which swept out of his mouth. Their screeching came as pain cut into him anew.

His captors, Dave and Vic, were sitting nearby on upended boxes, eating kebabs. They gazed down at Mandrake. He was screaming.

"Shut it!" Dave said harshly, shoving at him with his foot. He turned to Vic. "Get him to shut it." Vic went to the car which was parked at the far end of the warehouse. Between the screams, his footsteps scraped and tapped through the dust. After rummaging around in the boot, he took an oily rag and went to tie it over Mandrake's mouth.

Mandrake smelled the oil. He smelled the man without mercy. He opened his mouth to scream again, but no vocal sound would come. His breath rushed out bringing only a forced, primal hiss. Vic covered Mandrake's open mouth with the cloth. Roughly, he rolled him over to make a knot. Mandrake struggled.

"Get over here!" Vic shouted to Dave, who came and put his foot on the small of Mandrake's back, pushing down with a jerk and pinning him to the floor. Vic finished tying the gag. They left him lying on his front in the dirt.

Near the car, a small side door swung open briskly. A woman entered.

"Where is he then?" demanded Blanche as she walked towards them down the length of the building. She was wearing a dark, short skirted suit. Her legs flashed palely as she strode through the lamp beams. She was small and slight with tight black hair. She was pretty, but there was a wire around her heart which pulled her into tension. This tension made her feet move quickly. Her shoes clacked on the flooring as she took charge. Dave nodded towards the corner where Mandrake lay. They had paid him no attention since they had gagged him. They had rolled joints, smoked and drifted. Blanche went to him.

"Get the gag off," she said. Vic unwrapped Mandrake's mouth. The cloth was sodden with his dribble. Mandrake retched and then lifted his head unsteadily. He tried to sit up but he could not co-ordinate his body through the series of movements needed. His head drooped back to the floor, his forehead pressing into the grit.

"Turn him round", ordered Blanche. Dave and Vic dragged Mandrake across the floor and propped him against the wall, sitting in a pool of light, keeling over. Mandrake put out his arm, locking his elbow to make a prop, despite the way his hand seemed to be endlessly slipping away from him. Blanche stood in front of him, legs and arms akimbo.

"Now," she said, "I've got you. No more running for you. No more waiting for me. What have you got for me?"

"Nothing. Got nothing. Need some gear."

"I don't want any of your disgusting junk. Why did you go to Vienna?" Through his haze, Mandrake was surprised by this question. He had thought himself to be caught by dealers. Involuntarily, his free hand moved towards his throat and came to rest on his chest. He felt the key under his shirt, hanging from the light chain around his neck. Blanche saw. She stepped forward. Mandrake gripped the key.

"If you want this get me a fix." Blanche seemed to soften.

"What have you got there, Mandrake? Is it a souvenir from Vienna? Something to do with your winnings?" She stooped beside him, looking suddenly inelegant in her tight skirt, unable to kneel without danger of laddering her tights. "Jacket, Vic," she demanded, clicking her fingers. She knelt beside Mandrake on the jacket. "Tell me."

"It came from the girl. It fell from her pocket. Can't find the chest. Score for me. Please!" he begged. His eyes were screwed shut and his head waved to and fro in despair. Mandrake flinched as Blanche put her cold hand inside his shirt. She felt the tip of the key where the chain ran through the hole at the top.

For years she had paid little heed to this loser, looking elsewhere for her quarry. She had been successful in other fields, but in this case, she had drawn a blank. Never mind if he couldn't find the chest, he was just a junkie. She was Blanche with her special abilities. The chest was esoteric,

70

of that she was sure, and so the need for the true key was paramount. If this was it around his neck, she wanted it.

"Show me your key," she said, "then I'll get you what you want." Clumsily, Mandrake dragged it out. Blanche leaned forward, bringing up her hand in eagerness, ready to take. She could feel her heart beating faster, the crust of self-discipline cracking as desire leapt. When the key emerged, she balked, disbelieving. It was shiny, modern and completely ordinary. She snatched it from his hand, breaking the chain against his skin and then flung it away from her. A tiny clink sounded as it landed on the far side of the warehouse, muted by dust.

Blanche stood up, looking down at Mandrake. Her face had regained its hardness. Her eyes were stones. Mandrake looked up.

"Where's my gear?" She kicked his arm away from him and he lurched to the floor, landing twistedly, staring up at her, pleading.

"Get it yourself." Her indifference to him was chilling. Mandrake vomited. He tried to move away from the mess. Vomit ran from his sagging mouth. He choked, straining for his breath. His body forced him to cough again and again, pumping out precious air, unable to suck it back in through his scalding throat. Blanche turned to look at the men. Moments passed as the fit of choking ebbed. They gazed down from behind their barricades of dope.

"He's on his way out." She stepped back, roughly pushing him onto his side with her foot in its pointing shoe. Mandrake coughed weakly and then wheezed. "Let's go." She began to walk away, the men following her. Dave looked back. He could see Mandrake's feet trailing out of the shadow which hid his body in its depths. He felt shocked by what had almost happened, by what Blanche was assuming would happen.

"Junkie bastard," he sneered, but later, he called an ambulance and got the worry of it out of his head.

CHAPTER EIGHTEEN
Clive Admits Bruce

While Clive and Bruce waited for Mary, they sat quietly at first, sipping whiskies. Clive leaned back into the comfort of an arm chair. The cushions smelled slightly of dog. He was not surprised. If he was a dog, he would get onto this chair whenever he could. He gazed down at his trousers. They were shiny, baggy at the knees and worn. The cuffs of his cardigan were threadbare and, in this light, clearly grubby. He noticed a splash mark from some tea he had spilled yesterday. He felt lonely.

"Have you got time for this?" Bruce asked. "Were you due to be somewhere else, you know, Saturday night and all?"

"Saturday nights are not all they used to be," said Clive. "I had nothing planned and anyway, if I had, I'd have put it off in the light of all this."

"What do you think all this is?" said Bruce.

"Let's wait for Zorcia," said Clive.

"For who?"

"For Mary," said Clive, as if stating the obvious.

"I thought you said another name, like Chalker or something."

"Did I?" He paused. "Did I say…"

"Go on," said Bruce. Clive was thoughtful and then he seemed to reach a decision. Drawing in his breath, he said,

"Did I say Zorcia?"

"Yes. That's probably it. Zorcia, Chalker, they sound alike. Who's Zorcia then? You're long lost love?" Bruce cringed inside as the words left his lips. What had he said that for?

He felt clumsy and he blushed, trying to think of something better to say.

"Yes, she is if you'd like to know," said Clive, taking Bruce aback. In all the time that he had known Clive, although they had never been close, no hint of this had ever been given. All Clive's talk was of trivia, gossip, anecdote and easy opinions. There was never anything deep, engaging or personal. Nothing was shared. It was all on the surface, keeping himself out of reach but now, there was a change. Something was being offered.

"Tell me," said Bruce, relieved at the hope of redeeming himself after his tactlessness. "Tell me about Zorcia."

Clive shifted in his chair. He leaned back and crossed his legs, put down his whiskey and folded his arms, pausing to think. Then he sighed, uncrossed his legs and leaned forward, taking up the whiskey again and drinking it all. He cupped the glass in his hands. His demeanour changed, softening as he lowered his guard. Kindness showed clearly in his face. Still he did not speak. Bruce took Clive's glass and topped it up.

"I'd very much like to hear," he said, smiling gently down as he handed the glass back to Clive and enjoying the feeling of newly emerging friendship.

For the first time ever, Clive told of his meeting with Zorcia. Bruce listened with full attention and Clive could sense it. His tale was being truly heard.

"And I suppose you never saw her again," he stated when Clive had finished.

"I did see her again. If we'd never met again, I think I'd have just let it all go. It wouldn't have got such a hold on me. But we did meet again, in another place, beyond coincidence. Later that same summer, the yacht I was crewing came into Dubrovnik. I had only a brief time ashore before we were to go on to Greece. I just wandered around the town, love-sick for Zorcia and wishing that things were different.

"I turned into a whole lot of narrow, side-streets. You probably know the sort of thing you find in old cities, with

73

a network of homes, tiny shops, people, washing hung high across the street - life with a capital 'L'. I was drawn into a shop selling cloth. To this day I struggle with the law of probability and yet, at the time, it seemed the most natural thing in all the world."

"What? What was it?"

"She was in there, behind the counter." Bruce leaned forward eagerly.

"How come? How could she be? What did you do?"

"Of course we recognised each other and although we couldn't believe the situation, we accepted it. We were very happy, very joyful. She took my arm and led me out of the shop into the sun. She locked it up, laughing and shrugging. I guess she was supposed to stay but she didn't seem to care. I wanted to know how she had got there. I mean, if she had been a bus ride from Split the last time and now was in Dubrovnik, how come? I knew that whatever had happened, Zorcia was all right about it.

"It was something to be with her again. We walked out of the town, up the hills beyond. It was very hot. We sat in a field and looked down on Dubrovnik, through trees. We were together, close.

"Zorcia is the only woman I have ever loved. She came with me to the port. The attraction between us was electric. I felt real and alive. I knew with every bone in my body that we were meant to be together." Clive was leaning forward, his glass held in the palm of a hand, absent-mindedly weighing it, his face enchanted by memory. "Bruce, I can't tell you how beautiful she was, and she loved me. I didn't want to lose her.

"Then I did a stupid thing. I persuaded her to come back to the yacht with me. The long and the short of it was that she trusted me with more than I was able to give. I mean, she was full of knowing, yet she was also innocent. We knew we should be together, but running away like this was crazy! I was not powerful enough to protect her. All I could think about was that if we were parted now, we might never find each other again. This was like a second chance.

"When Zorcia was discovered, they put her ashore in Titograd. The owner had a meeting there. The skipper had said that Zorcia would go ashore as soon as possible and the opportunity came up very soon. I couldn't stop them. Nothing was negotiable. In my way I was also innocent. When I look back at that time, I'm sure I was working for gangsters. The whole set-up had a dodgy feel to it.

"People were flown off in a helicopter. There was no space for me and no co-operative feeling towards either of us anyway. I had to watch her being taken from me to be dumped, a great distance from her home village, a woman-child. Some of the crew had a whip-round and gave her a few clothes and money. I grabbed my handkerchief from my pocket and scrawled our initials on it with a biro but in the end, she was gone.

When they returned without her, we sailed on down the coast of Albania. In those days of course, we didn't stop there. She was completely out of reach."

"But it was so irresponsible," exclaimed Bruce.

"I know," said Clive." I've never stopped thinking about it."

"No, I don't mean you," Bruce said. "I mean the captain. Okay, you did a daft thing, but you were both very young. The captain made it much worse by what he did."

"To him she was just a dispensable peasant."

"Didn't her great beauty captivate them?" Bruce asked with a hint of mockery. Clive flinched and Bruce felt shame. Why do I say such stupid things, he wondered. "Sorry Clive," he muttered.

"Some people," replied Clive, "can't see what is right before them, can they?" Bruce blushed and could not find the next prompt. Mary came in.

"Would you like a whiskey?" Bruce asked her.

"Yes," she said. "I'd like a socking great whiskey, the stiffer the better." Bruce, looking surprised, began to get up to fetch her one. "However," she added, "I can't stand the smell or the taste of it, so it will give me no pleasure or relief." She looked at the ceiling where footfalls trickled across on the other side. "Those two I shall leave for a bit," she added, "but a large glass of good wine would just about hit the spot. Have we got any? Something fresh, white and uplifting?"

"There is a miracle of wine such as you describe in the fridge," said Bruce. He went to get it. Mary sank into a chair, stretching out her legs, kicking off her shoes and releasing the tension from her shoulders. Her hair, tousled and damp from bath and bed time, now rested as best it could, framing her face.

"Have you talked?" she asked.

"Yes, but not about today," said Clive, as Bruce returned with a large goblet for Mary. The footsteps above had stopped. Peace began to descend upon the home.

"Well," Mary said, "now we can talk."

CHAPTER NINETEEN

Zorcia Steps Out

On their approach to Titograd, Zorcia had been instructed not to look and she had spent the last five minutes of the journey with her head held down by one of the crew. They landed in a field where she was handed over to a man-servant in order that she be escorted off the huge property. She was led away across lawns and down an avenue of trees.

Near the gates, a tall hedge grew on the inside of the perimeter wall, making a pathway. Pausing at the mouth of the path and indicating secrecy, the servant beckoned her to follow him. Zorcia felt his kindness and walked behind him in trust. Besides, she had nowhere else to go. Eventually the hedge petered out. They walked quickly through a yard of farm buildings and out-houses. Geese hissed at their heels as they picked their way over worn and messy grass.

He took her to the kitchens. People were busy catering for the meeting. No one paid any attention as Zorcia was given food and tea. She wasn't hungry. She was too lost to want to eat. She put her hand into her pocket, comforted by the soft cloth of Clive's last, desperate gesture.

Suddenly behind her, one of the women knocked a stack of saucepans and vegetables sending them cascading to the stone floor. The crash was terrific and then people began to shout. The noise of the clear-up put people on edge. Tempers frayed.

"Get to the store and fetch some more! Do I have to think of everything?" a woman yelled at Zorcia, cuffing her in the direction of the cellar stairs. She had assumed Zorcia to be extra hired help for the occasion. Her friend nodded to Zorcia's enquiry and she set off. For now, she had work. She would eat and be sheltered.

Zorcia had left her village after the visit from the students. Her cousin Stojanka had persuaded her to follow them. Discontented with her life and enchanted by rumours of freedom, she had caught a glimpse of something utterly desirable when Mick and his friends had pulled into her village. As she saw their van disappearing, she resolved to follow them that very night.

When Zorcia understood what Stojanka intended, she decided to go too. She thought of the trouble that had always surrounded her cousin and wanted to help her and somewhere inside herself, she felt that she was being called away.

By walking through the night, they arrived in Split in time to locate Mick's van. It was parked up while his gang shopped. By the time they returned, the girls were settled into the back, smiling, indicating with their hands that they were there for a ride onward. The romance of being joined by two locals pleased the students immensely. This was their dream, to encounter real people and experience the essence of their host country. As they set off from Split, they smiled at one another and spoke little.

Each one of these young people had no experience of life without the ultimate protection of their elders. They followed their wishes but their mettle, as a personal resource, remained untested.

For Stojanka, this was liberation. Here she was, moving out fast. She had felt the frustration of boundaries all her life and now here was a change, a chance. It had to be better than life in the village. Zorcia had a different view. She sensed the limited quality of the interaction between all the members of the group. She could not understand what they said and she felt that they were play acting. She felt the tensions that coiled between them.

Stojanka pointed out to Zorcia all the things that she admired; the camping cooker, the quantity of books, the colourful tins of food, the clothes. She was excited by them. She felt closer to accessing these things for herself.

Very quickly, a sexual attraction was aroused between Stojanka and Pete, which exploded into uninhibited and noisy appeasement of their appetites at all possible and some almost impossible moments.

"Now I am different," Stojanka told Zorcia. "It changes you, you'll see," she claimed, assuming. Zorcia smiled, causing Stojanka to give her a second look which began with disbelief and finished with a dismissal.

By the time they reached Dubrovnik, Zorcia was ready to leave them. Stojanka seemed to beg her to stay, but they were already apart. Besides, Zorcia had no role within the confines of the cluttered van. Often, her mind returned to her lover beneath the breeze blown trees. Whatever it was that these three couples were going through, it was not the same thing at all.

Stojanka had confidence in something new. Zorcia did not share this confidence and believed that Stojanka would soon be needy again. For now, it was better for them to part. She felt unhesitatingly drawn to stay in Dubrovnik. And so she met Clive again and although the consequences of this meeting were that she became roughly tossed upon the sea of life, who can say that it would have been any different otherwise?

CHAPTER TWENTY

Zorcia Is Touched By Fear

The house in Titograd where Zorcia worked was a busy household, with many visitors and the staff to attend them. There came a day when the two daughters of the household were preparing for a holiday. Despite the regime existing in Yugoslavia then, families of this type could arrange time away in the luxurious haunts of the high profile rich. They were to go to Vienna to enjoy a series of concerts and balls. Zorcia and her fellow servant Jelena were to accompany them.

There was a lot of luggage to take to the station which proved to be the subject for much teasing of the two excited girls. Family, friends and servants gathered round the cars to wish them well. Zorcia, at the back and waiting to get into the last car, watched the final two trunks being loaded. She became aware that there was someone standing unnaturally close to her. She turned. It was Jovan, the head servant. He clasped her by the elbow and she could not pull away from him.

Jovan was powerful and influential within the workings of the household and he was not a good man. He wore a kind of uniform. The gossip was that he had designed, ordered and paid for it himself. The jacket, deep maroon and rather woolly, was fitted at the waist with a military cut. The matching trousers, straight legged over soft-soled, dull black shoes, emphasised his thinness and height. Why his black hair was tolerated, tied into a limp pony tail to reveal his shadowed eyes and fading youth, no one knew.

"That one," he pointed at one of the trunks. "You make sure it gets to Vienna. You make sure it stays with the rest of the luggage. You make sure that each time you change trains, it comes with you. You make sure of it."

Jovan was threatening her. He was so close. His hand pinched at her elbow. His breath invaded hers, forcing the odour of beer and onions into her nostrils. Some part of her drifted up, looked down at herself and felt calm. At the same time Jovan, by his presence, insisted that she be filled with fear. She was. A question began to form in her mind.

"Don't question me!" Jovan hissed. "Just do as I say." He released her elbow and turned towards the house. He passed before her and with his index finger, long and vicious, he jabbed her breast and then pinched it hard in a movement so swift that pain came suddenly.

The only other time that her breasts had been touched by another had been in love. She had now been assaulted whilst in a crowd. Her heart pounded. Friends came to say goodbye, but she was separated from them by fear. She could see them looking at her with concern. She tried to act normally and found that she could not remember how to do it. As she got into the car, another wave of fear broke over her, bringing a rim of sweat around her hairline and to the edges of her mouth. Fear is what separates us all from one another. This is the germ that causes all the playacting. At that moment, the force and the strength of it were all that Zorcia could feel.

As the party pulled away to cries of good wishes, waving hands and cheers, Zorcia joined in mechanically. From a window up in the servant's quarters, a curtain flicked. She thought that she caught a glimpse of Jovan's face, gaunt, shadowed and then suddenly withdrawn.

CHAPTER TWENTY-ONE

Zorcia Enters Choppy Water

During the journey, Zorcia obeyed Jovan's instructions. She watched all the luggage on and off the trains. She would have done this anyway. Engulfed in this strange new way of living, she feared the trunk would be lost and she feared its presence. She did not want to touch it, yet each time that she saw it she felt not only relief, but also dread, renewed. Since Jovan's violation of her, she had tried to wash him away, but the tiny quantity of water available on the train made it impossible for her to feel cleansed of the web in which he had placed her.

For Zorcia, the journey to Vienna was exhausting. The girls, full of pleasure at everything, drained her. She could not keep her mind from thoughts of the trunk. At first she made trips down the long corridor to the luggage van, until she realised how much attention she was attracting. She decided to stop. Jelena could not cheer her troubled friend, whose eyes began to sink.

In Vienna, the party was to stay with family friends. They were met at the station and taken to a huge house near the centre. Zorcia, along with the other servants, was driven to the back of the mansion. As they began to unload the cars, a man, wiry, clean shaven and dressed in a blue velvet suit and black, three-cornered hat, came forward. He took Zorcia by the wrist and spun her so that her back was to the others. He gripped the middle button of her blouse and began to pull and twist it. Down her front, he stuffed a piece of paper.

"Pay attention to this," he ordered, leaving quickly as Jelena approached them.

"Who was that, Zorcia?" she asked.

"I don't know." Zorcia was shaking and her blouse was unbuttoned. Gently, Jelena did it up for her.

"What has happened to you Zorcia? Tell me." Zorcia looked Jelena in the eyes and her own filled with tears. She could not speak. She turned and ran away over the cobbled yard and down some steps into the basement of the house.

She was sure that she would find a disused room there. Big houses always had these spare places with rooms that came into their own just occasionally. Zorcia went through the door at the bottom of the steps. It led into a long corridor which extended to her left and her right. The floor was stone and the walls shabby and bare. Down to her left, she heard voices calling instructions. She could hear the familiar clatter of a kitchen. At the same moment, she heard foot-falls coming down the steps behind her. She dashed to the right as fast as she could, her movements hushed.

Alert for silence within one of these rooms, Zorcia passed the doors. She heard the handle of the entrance door turning at the very moment that she found another door ajar, hinting at the solitude she sought. In a trice she went inside. She tried to close the door behind her, but it stuck on the uneven floor.

Zorcia stood behind the door, taking in as much air as she could in order to slow her breathing. Her chest felt tight. She wanted to cry and gasp. Instead, she listened through the thumping of the blood in her neck and the ringing of dread in her ears. Someone came into the basement but went off towards the kitchens. She could hear nothing more. Her knees were weak and her thighs shaking. She let herself sink to the floor.

Zorcia looked around the room. It was exactly what she had anticipated. This room would only be used in the coldest winter months. It was small, with a tiny barred window high up on the external side. The walls were bare, apart from a series of rough hooks from which were slung an assortment of toboggans, skis, poles, boots and skates. Mildew and rust dusted some of the older pieces. The air was musty, thick with late autumn heat. The room was clearly forsaken.

The note, scrunched and sharp, rustled. Zorcia took it out. A key fell from the paper.

"Use this key. Take the contents to this address. Do as you are told." In alarm, Zorcia remembered the trunk. The luggage was being unloaded now and she was not there to manage it. She leapt up and ran back to the yard. As she came to the top of the basement steps, it seemed to be deserted. In the shadow of a wall lay the trunk. She paused in time to see two men approaching it with caution. Their bodies were tense. They tried to look casual, but they were stiff with concentration.

For the first time since her encounter with Jovan, Zorcia felt her head clear. She walked into the yard, making a successful attempt to look at home. She walked up to the men and gestured at the trunk. She smiled at them, forcing some kind of warmth into her eyes. Then she turned to look up at the house and waved. When she turned back, the men were running away. Jelena came out.

"Where have you been?"

"Never mind," said Zorcia. "Help me move this over there." She had grabbed a handle at one end of the trunk and gestured towards the basement. Jelena took the other end and they staggered across the yard with the awkward burden. She looked at Zorcia, full of questions, yet asked nothing more.

They moved the trunk into the skate room. If they were seen, no one showed any interest in two servants performing an ordinary looking task.

"Jelena, thank you for helping, but please leave me alone now. Please leave me alone and say nothing. If I need more help, can I ask you? Can you agree to say nothing? There is danger, but I don't understand anything more than that. We will both be safer if you can help in this way."

"Such mystery," said Jelena, "of course I will help you." She left the room, pulling the door hard behind her. The loose flagstone tipped, the door slid over it and jammed shut. Zorcia rushed to the door to open it, but the flagstone had rocked back and was wedged against the door. She called after Jelena. Her voice came thinly from her taut throat and could not penetrate the thickness of the wooden door.

Zorcia turned to the trunk and taking the key from her pocket, she unlocked it and lifted the lid which was awkward and bowed in the middle. Tired air drifted out. Inside, something large was packed in with old cotton wadding. Zorcia sniffed at it and picked out a small clump. The wadding tickled her nose, only smelling of itself. She pushed her hand down in to it, feeling her way.

Pulling aside the packing, Zorcia found a curving surface. It was the lid of a small chest made from dark and ancient leather. It was worn with scratches, dented and frayed at the corners and was securely fastened by a padlock that seemed to have no keyhole. It was engraved with twirls and stars on either side.

CHAPTER TWENTY-TWO

How Mandrake Came To Lose His Home

By the time Mandrake was found by the ambulance crew, he was close to death. Apart from the shock to his whole body system that occurs during withdrawal from an addictive substance, he had inhaled vomit.

The crew were compassionate and practical men. They were experienced in their work and had witnessed more human vulnerability than most people. Here before them on the cold hard ground, lay a man in desperate need and danger. They did all they could for him and then lifted him onto a stretcher with infinite tenderness, taking him to the hospital and delivering him to the accident and emergency team.

The hospital was old, white tiled and with some kind of hard flooring that magnified every sound. Each dropped item, each squeaking wheel, each voice contributed to the echoes resounding within the rooms. The team worked quietly, but the noises were raw.

Two young nurses walked by the open doors. They were imitating their nurse tutor, unfairly as it happened, putting on a fussy, authoritarian voice.

"This room stinks! What is the cause of it? See to it at once!" The words, distinct, shot in through the emergency room doorway. Mandrake tensed. For all that was happening, for all that he could not speak, or see, or control his body, his hearing was acute and in his confusion, he heard this admonishment not in jest but for real. For years after he had been taken into care, the matron of his children's home had consistently failed to convey to him that she meant him no personal harm. Stating facts and then dealing with them as swiftly as possible was, for her, simply practical. She had no idea of the effect her words might have on someone else.

86

After Gwendolyne's death, Mandrake's household had not lasted long. Without her, the strong centre of the family taken from them so completely and so horrifically, his parents had reverted to their former way of life. It took little more for the children to be taken away.

A new baby had been born to them soon after the brutal accident. The birth was long and difficult. Depression, barely at bay after the loss of her mother, fell upon Sheila once again. Colin tried to manage for them all, but he could not stand the relentlessness of the baby's demands, or the passive misery of his wife. Drinking quickly soothed him whenever he caught a glimpse of the depth of their difficulties. Nothing was going right at home and he did not know how to make it better.

In only a few weeks, the mess was worse. At every turn, the obstacles to putting things right seemed insurmountable. At the pub, only a handful of men would choose to drink with Colin and he, sensing pity, was too proud to drink with most of them. He liked Ronnie though, who could drink at the same pace as he and with the same concentration. He never ducked out or suggested that Colin had had enough and should be getting home.

Sometimes, Ronnie's wife Molly would come to fetch him from the pub. They had a stack of children. Colin didn't know how many. Molly was tender and firm with them all, including Ronnie. He always went with her without hesitation, apart from finishing his pint. Colin liked that, the way that Molly was. Her eyes always had something to say that was interesting. Even when she was under pressure, they never dimmed with self-pity.

Now take Sheila. Where had her spirit gone? None of them could reach her, not even the new baby. He thought of her when Robin, their first child and son, had been born. Her eyes had been misty with love for one and all at that time. It warmed his heart to recall their joy and then it twisted in pain to think of how things had changed. Colin gulped his beer. He drank to the bottom of his glass and ordered more. If he drank enough, it would wash these thoughts away.

He looked at the sawdust on the floor, scuffing it with his boot. When he lifted the new glass to his mouth, his hand shook enough to make a spill. The beer splashed over his hand, running uncomfortably along his forearm, down to his elbow inside his sleeve, irritating him. He leaned over his pint and sucked the beer up. Despite his hopes for oblivion, his thoughts returned to Sheila.

Why couldn't she be strong like Molly or Gwendolyne? Why was she leaving it all up to him? Why didn't she want him? What did she want? He didn't know what to do with kids. For a start, the baby wanted her, not him.

When he lifted her up, little Mary, he felt so clumsy. When she cried, he felt her push him away as if he were an obstacle to the meeting of her needs. He could not feed her or comfort her like a mother. He just wanted to make things right for them so that Sheila could look after them all properly.

Look at Robin now. He was pretty well silent unless talking to Mandy. His big, brown eyes just looked and looked. They looked like wise eyes, but Robin didn't know how to run a home. Anyway, he was a boy and Mandy too young and weak to help her mother much.

Colin felt that he was surrounded by weakness and it made him feel weak too. When Gwendolyne had been around it had been all right, but now, without her strength he could not find his own. If he drank enough of it, beer dumbed down his despair. Colin drained his glass and called for more.

He spent as little time as possible at home. It wasn't what he meant. He intended to be there more, tidy around and do the garden perhaps, keep things nice enough. But when he awoke in the morning, his head thick and thumping, with no one to look after him and a house full of needy people, he just wanted to get out for a bit. He wanted time to think things through and decide what to do for the best. He wanted a hot meal, peaceful happy sounds around the home, warmth, a lover. He would go out again.

Without Gwendolyne there to give a welcome, neighbours soon stopped calling. Her death had stunned the village community and the nation beyond. At first, the family received heartfelt sympathy, letters, toys, second hand clothes, flowers, but Colin was difficult for people to relate to. Awkwardness took over, quickly followed by assorted excuses to forsake good intentions made in shock.

Only Slater's wife, Ruth, came to the Birch household. She was now living away from her marital home, renting a small cottage which looked out over the village green. She had no intention of returning to her husband, whatever the outcome of his trial should be. She did not want to go back to their house of lies. Lucy and she had set up their own secure haven and were more relaxed, happy and friendly than she could ever have believed possible.

Ruth had discovered a source of inner strength that she had sensed, but not known how to reach. All those years of compliance to a bully! She could not regret them; she had her children and she had discovered so much, although she was aghast at how long it had taken her to fetch up a sufficient head of steam to see through a change.

Now she felt bound to help the Birchs both because of her developing personal beliefs and because of her connection with the death. On many days, Ruth went to help in the house. She liked to be there as long as Colin was out. She wanted to love him, her neighbour, but in relation to his drinking, he reminded her too much of Gerald. Colin didn't do the same things as him, but he was still messing up his life by the same method. Her wounds in that respect were too fresh for her to be in the presence of either man.

If Ruth saw Colin pass her kitchen window on his way to the pub, she would leave her own chores and go up to Sheila, knowing that she had a clear two hours before Colin would be anywhere near to considering his return home. Once there, she would tend to Mary, cook for the family and clean a little.

Ruth could see how much Colin also needed help, yet she could not bring herself to give it. She prayed that she could find a way, but the reason that she did not was simple - she didn't really want to, so nothing could change. After so many years of submission, each time she contemplated helping this weak man, her mind rebelled and she would not let him into her heart. When Colin began to stay at home, drinking, immobilised in his chair, Ruth was unable to go there any more.

She had always done her best to be good. This had taken the form of fulfilling her role as wife and mother with a cheerful and accommodating spirit. She had not been raised to put her own needs in her sights. Throughout her childhood and adult years, she had been given to understand that her privileged position in society negated her own needs or interests. Thus, during all this time, if she ever felt something uncomfortable or distressing, she dismissed it and jollied herself along. The very idea that she could need something for herself, could choose something just for her on her own account, could not enter her head. There had been no entrance into her mind for such a concept.

Now, looking back, all those years seemed like a lie between herself and life. She read the Bible, trying to discover how to be true, but it seemed so complicated. She knew that it was one of God's commandments that she should love her neighbour, but the next phrase, to love her neighbour as herself, explained why she could not go to the aid of Colin and his family any more. She did not love herself, not enough and not consistently. She rang the social worker and said that she was pulling out.

CHAPTER TWENTY-THREE

Mary Moves On Into Safekeeping

Mary, a tiny baby, was swiftly put up for adoption. The papers were prepared, court orders made and she was swept away from her birth family into the all-embracing care of Hugh and Clarissa. After two decades of childless marriage, their life abruptly and completely changed.

Their home had been as empty as Clarissa's womb. There had been no joyful swelling of her belly, no choosing of nursery wallpaper, no uncomfortable sleep, no gradual adjustments as a child approached their lives. After years of longing, disappointment and vetting, Mary was given to them one Tuesday afternoon. They took her home and she began to become their daughter.

Each day, their home filled more and more with Mary's presence. Hanging on the back of a chair, Hugh found a little, cream vyella dress. He lifted it to his face, smelling the soapy freshness and feeling the soft cloth against his closed eyelids. His heart sang with purpose. Gently, he put back the little dress, relishing the years before him that would bring other moments as precious as this.

When Clarissa came into the room, carrying Mary against her shoulder, Hugh adored the top of her warm little head, fluffy with dark hair. He kissed her fontanel. Her tiny, tender hand clutched at a fold on Clarissa's jersey, the other arm extended under her new mother's chin. Mary gazed at her smiling new father, recognised him and beamed. He took her in his arms and he could not help but sing. His voice was sweet for her and he sang with a pure and passionate love.

"I hear the cotton fields whisper above, Daddy, Daddy, Daddy's in love."

CHAPTER TWENTY-FOUR

Mandrake Moves On

Robin and Mandy were put into foster care with the Sheppys. They were kind, but the family of nine, a mixture of natural and fostered children, was rough and ready. It was noisy and busy. There was no place to be quiet. Robin, already nervous, never felt calm. Anxiety riddled him constantly. He cried easily, whined often and wet the bed at least once every night. During the day, he would hold on for too long and then have further accidents. The Sheppys were used to children coming and going. Robin went. While he awaited his new placement, he was to live in a children's home.

At Sunnyfields, he was put into a dormitory of twenty boys ranging from five to fifteen. He would not speak except to say, 'Mandy'. He was pale. He was small, thin and easy to push around. Everyone seemed to be in a rush. They seemed to know what to do. Robin could not work out how to join in appropriately. No one rescued him with guidance or protection. Being with people hurt. He tried to keep away from them.

Sunnyfields was a huge sprawling house. It had begun as a family home and over time had changed hands and been extended, always in an ungainly way. Robin, excellent quarry that he was for bored, insecure boys, had discovered many nooks in which to hide in this rambling place.

He felt safest in the basement in a series of cluttered, damp rooms, bare brick walled and poorly lit. Robin was able to creep into the smallest of places and to remain utterly still for such a long time, that his raucous hunters could not usually sustain their interest.

He would crouch in fear of being found, keeping silence as the search took place. The sound of running feet and noisy whispers would come close, but so far he had not been found in this complex place. Besides, it was at around this time that the home employed Mr Jopply as handy-man.

One Saturday afternoon, Jopply rescued Robin who had tucked himself in behind a heap of abandoned tools. Jopply had noticed an old woodlathe as he had been shown around the basement when he came for the job. He had ear-marked it for a project to pursue on quiet days and on this rainy day, as Robin hid, Jopply made his way to the lathe. He approached from the northern end of the basement, walking quietly down the passage as was his way. He was hidden in the shadows. From the other end charged a crowd of shouting boys.

"Mandy! Mandy! Mandy!" they chanted, as they began to hunt their quarry in one of the rooms. They were high on the chase, feeling the power of the gang and sharing a determination to find Robin no matter what. Matron was off-duty and they felt freed into unruliness. They began to pull junk out of the rooms and into the corridor.

Robin could not escape this time. As they heaved out the heavy old tools, he could feel the floor vibrating and he too, shook. As a little more light was cast towards him, he began to scream. He could not stop. All around him on the floor, the warm, wet of his fear began to chill on the flagstones.

"Now we know you! Now we know you!" In their hurry, the gang surged forward, heedless of their own safety. One of them stepped onto a hay-rake which smashed up into his face. His stunned silence fleetingly spread to the whole group and was broken as blood spurted from his nose and forehead. Cries of pain and shock came from his mouth.

Into this came Jopply, a practical man, who swiftly enabled the boys to disperse, urging them to take their wounded friend to the under-matron without delay. He kept himself between them and the tiny, haunted boy. When they had gone, he knelt down beside Robin who was hunched into a cave of junk. Planks of dusty splintering wood, rusty piping and cracked hardboard leaned over him, propped against the damp, distempered wall. He could smell the urine, stale and fresh. He felt it soaking through his trouser knees, but that was just background information. His attention was caught by Robin's slightness of form, his downcast eyes and his thin little arms around his bony, square knees.

Jopply knew what it was to be hunted. He had experienced it during the last war and he had been caught by his enemies. He was not at war with this little boy. How could he show him that he was safe? Gently he pulled away, stood up and began to quietly sort through the piles of abandoned things. He sang softly as he worked.

"Lavender's blue, Dilly, Dilly, Lavender's green…" Time wore on. "Sugar in the morning, sugar in the evening, sugar at supper-time…" In the pauses he could hear the boy snuffling as he sobbed. He bent down again and gave him his handkerchief. The boy took it.

"What's your name then, son?" Jopply asked. "Is it Mandrake? Is that what they call you?" Robin said nothing and after that, because this kind man had made it so, Mandrake became his name and he answered to it.

CHAPTER TWENTY-FIVE

Zorcia Runs Close To Rocks

Zorcia pulled the chest out of the trunk. It was awkward and quite heavy. Something inside shifted slightly, as if loosely packed, although it made no sound. The light began to fade. There was a switch, but the bulb had gone. Zorcia turned her attention to getting out of the room. The only way to tip the flagstone down enough to open the door was to put all her weight on it and to use the handle as leverage, but as soon as she switched her strength to pull on the door, the stone flipped up again.

Frustration began to blind her. In her temptation to give in to it, the memory of Jovan broke through and she renewed her concentration. She was relieved that she did not know what the chest contained.

Zorcia looked on the tool shelf but found nothing there to help her. Over in a darkening corner, she found some ice-breaking tools, including a sturdy pick. At last she had a means to lever the stone. Motivated by her mounting alarm at this delay to her errand, she swung the stone right out of its socket and pulled open the door.

By now, the evening was settled. Lights had come on in the kitchens. The courtyard, lit only from various windows in the house, was mostly in darkness. Zorcia knew that the girls would have missed her well and truly by now, although Jelena would be doing her best to keep her covered. She had to get on and take the chest to the address she had been given.

In the dim light, she looked at the note again. She was to take it to a theatre. Whatever trouble she might be in with regard to her employer, she would have to deal with it later. Zorcia heaved the chest onto her hip and walked out into the streets of Vienna.

This was the first time in her life that she had been alone in this way. A foreigner, without the language, lost and under threat. How could she progress her errand?

The streets were wide and the buildings pleasing to her eye. Traffic whisked and jangled by, stirring city dust. The day was cooling as the evening advanced, bringing people out for their leisure. Zorcia joined them, walking along beneath the avenues of trees. Starlings flocked above in great whirls of constant motion. Where they clustered, the noise of their roosting was almost deafening.

The chest became increasingly difficult to carry and grew heavier with every step. Zorcia was looking for someone to whom she could show her piece of paper with the address. She felt bewildered. How was she supposed to complete this task? After the close shave with those two men in the afternoon, was she being watched now?

A group of people overtook her. They were animated, their arms linked in friendship. Zorcia signed to them, asking for help, hoping that they might even be heading for the same destination as her. Discussion took place within the group. Some sort of consensus was reached. They invited her to walk with them, offering to help her with her burden.

At a junction, they returned the chest to her, pointing Zorcia down a different street from the one that they were to take. Night had fallen and she filled with loneliness. The sky was clear and through the light pollution, she could see a small number of stars, so far away, shining down on her, on Titograd and her own home village all at once. Yet here on the ground, in this strange city, she was separated from all that she knew. Unsure that she could even find her way back to the house and Jelena, she longed for this task to be completed so that she could be free from the claim that it made upon her.

The crowds thickened. They helped her when asked. At last, Zorcia found the theatre, its name matching the words on the paper. People were meeting and greeting one another at the front, dressed warm and smart, expressing pleasured anticipation. Doormen dressed in blue velvet with three cornered hats, attended the gathering audience.

Seeing them, Zorcia halted at the edge of the throng. Her sudden cessation of movement caught the eye of one of the doormen as he looked up. Their eyes met. It was the man who had delivered the note. Zorcia's face formed a question to which he replied with a jerk of his head. Suddenly aware of her exhaustion, she slowly turned towards the back of the theatre and almost immediately felt the doorman's presence behind her. He began to take the chest from her. She was ready to relinquish it as she had so desired, but when she looked at his face she knew that he meant to do her harm.

Clutching the chest in reaction, she ran away from him, gaining strength from deep inside herself. She heard shouts which caused her to run harder. Although she was tired and encumbered, she quickly dodged through the crowd which closed behind her, slowing her pursuer. She turned down a passage and made for the only light that showed. It was neon, lighting up the words, Wien Nachts above a door at the bottom of some steps. She ran down these and fell against the door which swung open. She had staggered into a nightclub. The door was shut firmly behind her.

Her arrival caused a brief stir. It was unexpected and unusual after all. As a knocking sounded on the door behind her, she was swiftly led through the heart of the crowd and into an anti-room. She sat on red plush cushions scattered on ornately carved mahogany couches. The walls were covered with cream damask and decorated with gold framed paintings of men and women in Makart costumes, performing private acts. Above Zorcia, the ceiling mirrored her upturned face. Her ears rang from her exertion. Her throat tasted of blood and felt tight. She held the chest in her lap, panting.

Heavily tasselled curtains separated her from the night club where people were shouting so much that it sounded as if they might fight. Keeping hold of the chest, she stepped forward and peeped through the curtains. A theatre doorman, not the one she had seen before, was doing most of the shouting. By his gestures, Zorcia guessed that he was demanding to search for her there. Despite the fact that he was in no position to demand anything and that he was being manhandled by two tall, fat bouncers, he persisted. It was easy for them to turn him out. There was nothing that he could do to prevent himself from being hurled out of the door to land awkwardly on the steps outside, dignity abandoned. Renewed banging on the door was ignored and attention now focused on Zorcia.

CHAPTER TWENTY-SIX

Mandrake Tries An Escape Route

At Sunnyfields Mandrake lived as an abandoned child. For the duration of those hard years, the taciturn, bed wetting, disappointed child remained without further placement. In bed at night, beneath too few blankets, curled up tight, cold and still, he hovered between sleep and despair. In the dormitory, the sounds of lonely boys at night wore at him through the endless, chilling hours.

Mandrake kept himself apart. Being with people hurt, being without them hurt, but at least this total cut-off was up to him. He could control it. He gave nothing away; no meeting of eyes with the dinner lady who tried to mother him, no access to the student teacher who was sure she would make a break-through, no falling in with another lonely soul. Nothing. Unless there was a dare or a gamble. Then he could call the shots, participate and even lead. Such moments brought him his life, when he could abandon himself to these proscribed events, returning to withdrawal at their close.

When it was time to leave Sunnyfields, Mandrake had learned to play for reckless stakes. He had nothing to lose but the chance to participate. His life developed a swing between penury and luxury. At last he began to fall in with other lonely souls, committing himself to a network of extreme gamblers, cast over continents and intricately woven into the fabric of cities, towns and villages - maybe here, maybe there - wherever decreed by those who made the odds. It became his way of life.

CHAPTER TWENTY-SEVEN

Zorcia Hits Rocks

Hans Klimpt wanted power and influence and he wanted as much as he could get. He needed money - much more than conventional work alone could bring. In Wien Nachts, he instigated some serious gambling. Driven to ruthlessness by his desire for wealth, he took risks, pushing up the odds and often hitting a winning streak. He laid bets that others would not have considered.

When Zorcia had almost fallen in to Wien Nachts through the carelessly unfastened door, Klimpt had sized her up. She looked like a Yugoslav and probably couldn't speak German. The surprise in her eyes and her willing acceptance of shelter, betrayed her innocence. She had nothing between herself and him.

As Zorcia sat undefended, Klimpt ordered that she should be detained by the offer of food and drink. He gave particular instructions regarding the wine, and what else it should contain. Then he came up with his most outrageous suggestion yet. Because of the way she had been pursued, the chest that the girl carried was probably valuable. That was gamble number one. The girl herself was pretty enough to make gamble number two. Each of the six men at the table should put up a stake, the winner gaining all the money, the chest and the girl.

Those around the table, used to giving away nothing of their thinking, retained their expressionless faces. They were each unalike and from different walks, but united in their addiction to extreme gambling. A fleeting shadow passed across the face of the man opposite Klimpt, but even he did not demur. Giving grounds for loss of face would be the greatest error of all to make in this company. The basis for trust between them hinged upon their union in risk taking.

Klimpt was always able to attract fast players. His power and influence in Vienna earned him something beyond tolerance. His custom was desired because of the kudos that came in the wake of his wagers.

On the other side of the table, Mandrake waited for the cards to be dealt. Through the years he had mastered himself enough to hide his thoughts. At a glance, which was all that most people gave him, he appeared calm, stoic. In point of fact, he was thinking that this was an appalling situation. The girl looked about the same age that Mandy would be now. He always thought like that. He hoped that Herr Schwartz, the proprietor, would put a stop to what was happening because he knew that he did not have the power to do it himself.

Two of the other men made asides to each other about how they would use the girl. They leered over their fantasies, laughing together. Sweat broke out on their brows. Mandrake glanced up. Through a slit in the curtains, he saw a waiter delivering a selection of torte to the the girl.

Zorcia was very hungry. She let herself be looked after. She was warm and felt protected. The waiter was friendly, reassuring her when she indicated that she had no money. For the first time since she had left Titograd, she had an appetite. She relished all that was put before her, including the rich, red wine. Once or twice, she thought that she should be getting back to the house, but the unpleasantness of facing up to the disapproval that would surely meet her there and the luxury of what she was enjoying now, could not compare. All this comfort and warmth put her at her ease. Besides, she still had the chest to deal with and she did not want to think about it now.

Tension mounted at the gambling table. People did not gather round. This was a private matter. The atmosphere was heavy. Mandrake could see that Klimpt was sexually aroused. He felt disgust at himself and this situation. All he could do, was to win.

The cards on the table indicated that he was in with a chance. Klimpt could not prevent the gleam of greed from showing in his eyes. His cards were good and he was caught by expectation. Mandrake took his next card and was shocked by its excellence. He had won. He placed his cards in front of the others.

CHAPTER TWENTY-EIGHT

Mandrake Is Given Some Consideration

"What is it then?" asked Mary. "What's been going on?" Clive and Bruce leaned forward and Mary echoed them. Bruce began.

"I was just preparing to shut when Mandrake arrived. Actually, I'd already locked the door, but he looked persistent and so I let him in. Immediately, all this cloak and dagger stuff began. At first I didn't feel particularly bothered. I didn't think that it would affect me in any way. I just thought that he'd go away when I'd fed him, but he sort of dragged me into it. He made me hide behind the counter with him and it was soon obvious that he was running scared. He was a mess and nervous and I picked up on it.

"He muttered about being in trouble and something about getting some sort of winnings in Austria, but he never said any more at that point because it was then that his pursuers came by and we had to hide even more. I think it was around this time that Jenny phoned and then later, Mandrake let me call back. He was not threatening me with anything in particular, but he was being threatening and I just don't know the fighting shouting world that Mandrake occupies. I'd never be up to taking him on and I know it, so I was beginning to feel more and more frightened.

"When Mandrake decided that the men had gone, he said that I was to go with him and I felt I had no choice. It was like being hypnotised. He said, now this is the part that really got me going, he said that I possessed something of his and that he was going to get it back. It turned the whole situation on its head. There I was, feeding him, hiding him in my place, fully expecting him to move on and take his chaos with him. Suddenly, I was involved with no idea of where the goal posts were.

"I don't know what he could have meant by his words and behaviour towards me. Was he out to get the house back or what? If he was referring to the house, why? The sale went through well and there was never any wrangling about the price. You know how there is often some sort of bad feeling between vendor and purchaser during those times? Well, that just didn't happen with this sale."

"No, it didn't," said Mary. "I remember that at the time he seemed eager to be shot of it and he was surprisingly helpful. I say surprisingly because he usually seemed so awkward, as if life was always complicated and difficult for him. Well, what's happened this evening proves that. But he left the house empty, didn't he?" Bruce and Mary reflected on the empty rooms through which they had wandered on their arrival.

"There weren't even any old newspapers."

"Do you remember how the front door was left open when we got here?" asked Mary.

"That's a strange coincidence, considering our homecoming tonight," said Clive.

"Yes, but do you think that someone may have come in then and taken something, the whatever-it-is that Mandrake's going on about?" Mary asked.

"I think we're in danger of making too much of this," said Clive. "Mandrake may be capable of reason, but at the same time, he is a drug addict and that's a very hard place to be. As a hospital porter you get to see things. From the little I saw, he looked out of it this evening. He may even have muddled you with someone else."

"Well God help that someone else then, if that is so!" Bruce exclaimed.

"It seems that Mandrake himself needs God's help now," said Clive.

"Shouldn't we call the police?" asked Mary.

"Believe me," said Clive, "there's not enough for them to go on and they won't be remotely interested. We didn't get any descriptions of the people in the car, or even the number plate for that matter. They're not going to go to too much trouble over this one."

Mary was not entirely convinced by this, although she wanted to be. Bruce also felt that it was not the right place to stop trying. His mind began to clear.

"I've had such a fright that I didn't even think of it, but if it had been me being snatched away like that, I'd count on being rescued and expect the police to play a part. I'd hope and hope that at the very least a passer-by would inform them. We have a greater responsibility because we actually know Mandrake. It's not okay for me to do nothing. Although you could be right Clive, just think what may have happened to me if you hadn't done what you did. Now it's for me not to turn away." Bruce left the room to make the call.

Mary and Clive sat quietly. They could hear Bruce in the next room, making the intermittent noises of someone working their way through a chain of people and answer-phones. Then he began to talk to someone.

"Thank you for all this Clive," Mary said, more awkwardly than she wished. Clive nodded and half smiled.

"Your Bruce is a good man. He's good to be around. That's what makes High Table work. I'm not like that."

"Oh, but," Mary began to protest. Just now, she had no bearings regarding who was good or not. She was feeling uncomfortable, nagged by memories of Bruce and her running Clive down for being someone to avoid because of his ability to be so boring. The centre of a companionable nest, their home, was such an easy place to jeer from.

"It's okay," Clive said quickly, putting up his hand in a halting gesture. "I know I'm hard work. I keep people out. Bruce lets them in." Bruce came back into the room. Clive and Mary quizzed him with their eyes.

"I got through, eventually. I began to wonder if I should have dialled 999, but as we'd left it so long I thought it was a bit late for that. I don't know what may have been achieved, but at least they didn't make me feel a fool for trying. Perhaps it will help Mandrake. It feels better to have rung."

"Yes," said Clive. "It was right."

"Well," said Mary, "what now? Mandrake is who knows where, doing who knows what. I wonder if we'll ever find out or see him again."

"Only time will tell," said Clive.

CHAPTER TWENTY-NINE

Mandrake's Neighbour

Mandrake was very ill. He had much to overcome. To begin with, his will to recover was weak. His body suffered from many years of poor nutrition and the costly effects of drug addiction and severe emotional stress. His spirit was starved. The long-term lack of love in his life had worn him to the bone. Now in withdrawal, forcibly begun and ill with pneumonia, he was under serious pressure if he wanted to keep his life. He didn't think that he wanted it any more and began to let it go.

Mandrake was given all the care that the hospital team knew to give, but along with this care came their expectation of his death. Mandrake, deep into his departure, felt this and did not change his plans.

In the bed next to his, Bob Hodges was recovering from a stroke. Doctors called it mild. To Bob it felt catastrophic. He had kept his power of speech, yet he felt out of touch with his tongue and mouth and the words did not form easily or swiftly. Although he could still think, his concentration was affected and he found it difficult to stick to the point whether speaking or listening. He found himself distracted by details and would forget the content of a conversation in favour of a small piece of fluff on his dressing gown, or a bird sitting on the sill outside the window. It tried everyone's patience, including his own. He felt constantly indebted to all his carers and visitors and he worried that they would give up on him if he couldn't pick himself up.

Bob and Mandrake lay in their beds, two men in a bay of six. The other beds were empty, cleared this morning by patients going home and they now stood waiting, their starched sheets and grey covers, their wiped lockers and blank charts, for others to fare like him, one way or another, struck into the dependence of illness.

Bob looked at Mandrake in the next bed, helpless and needing every thing to be done for him. Sometimes he felt angry that this comparatively young man had let his life get to this point of waste. At others, he recognised that this man too would have a story bringing him to his current state. In spite of knowing that a stroke had killed and crippled many people, some of them far younger than himself, Bob could not feel fortunate. He guessed this man could not either.

Every day, he struggled to seem cheerful as he ran the gauntlet of tests, therapies and hospital meals. For all the attention that he received, he could not find a chink in any one's time that might enable him to talk about his feelings, for what he might hope or prepare himself. He was struck dumb with indulgence, with being tucked up in bed, with grapes, flowers, chocolates and soap and by the look in every person's eyes that begged him not to ask awkward questions or to speak of anything real. Bob's blood pressure began to rise and his medication was adjusted accordingly. Inside his chest he felt a burning, but he did not mention it to anyone. He felt certain that no pill could shift it.

When Bob saw how Mandrake was sinking, his noisy struggle for breath chipping at his own peace of mind through the lone hours, his own sense of panic increased. His ability to take in air felt tied to that of his neighbour.

That night, he felt the panic rising. For hours now he had felt so alone with his thoughts and with the witnessing of this man's struggle - this stranger whom no one named, who neither came into life nor went out of it. Suddenly he felt the pain of panic rush up to his head and burst out with his breath. He gasped as he took in the air and began to sob. He was beyond constraint. He could no more stop this than he could hold his hand in a flame.

He was in a tragedy, crying for himself, crying for the world, crying for all the bitter sorrows that he had ever witnessed - they all seemed to be the same thing. As he felt that his heart would break, he also felt the possibility of relief.

Bob longed for comfort, although he would rather be alone than be inflicted with empty platitudes. He knew that he was making a noise. He knew that someone would come. He ached for that someone. He dreaded that someone.

He felt a gentle hand upon his shoulder. No words were spoken. Then the person took their hand from his back and came round to sit beside him on his bed. Through his tear-filled eyes, shut tight in each spasm of sobbing, he could see the blue of a nurse's uniform. She took his hand. His nose ran.

"I'm sorry. I'm so sorry," he wept.

"Where does it hurt?" she asked. Her question took Bob's attention back to his body. He felt so much pain in his heart, his throat and around his shoulders where he had been straining to hold in the air to prevent himself from crying. Tension spun around his collar bone and up the back of his neck. It hurt all around there. His head throbbed. His stomach churned. Bob put his hands to his heart.

"Here," he said. "It hurts here, and my head and along here." He indicated his shoulders and throat and then moved to his stomach. "Here too," he said, before folding his hands back across his heart.

"Would you like me to help you by giving you some healing?" she asked.

"What do you mean? Do I have to move from here, do something odd? Are you going to do something odd?" asked Bob.

"It's very straight forward and I believe it will soothe you just now."

"Oh go ahead, anything that may help. Do what ever you think best. You're the nurse," he said. The nurse got up and stood behind Bob, putting her palms beneath his shoulder blades.

"Take a couple of slow breaths," she said. "Fill up here," and she cupped his ribs with her hands. As he breathed in, peace began to flood his body and he was able to cry with ease.

"I'm sorry," he said again, blowing his nose, wiping his eyes and covering his face with his hands.

"It's all right. It's good," she said, coming back to sit on the bed. "Let's be quiet together. I'll stay here for as long as I can. If you want to talk, that's fine too." She held his hand in both of hers for a moment and then rested hers upturned upon the bed, with his resting on top. It felt good to keep his hand there. A sense of calm that Bob had long, long forgotten, came into him and settled there.

CHAPTER THIRTY

Mandrake And Zorcia Are Cheated

When Mandrake put his cards on the table, Klimpt, who usually lost a gamble with apparent nonchalance, felt a flash of anger. He shoved the table towards Mandrake so hard that he was winded and pinned to his chair. Those nearby became quiet, turning towards the commotion. Further into the club the atmosphere was unaffected. Clicking his fingers, Klimpt jerked his head towards two men in the crowd. They immediately followed him.

Zorcia was slumped across the cushions. The wine waiter had followed his instructions. Klimpt and his men burst into the chamber. He pointed to Zorcia and he pointed to the chest, one man apiece. Then he spun on his heel and the men took up their bundles and followed him through a side door.

Klimpt led them down a brick lined corridor. The floor was damp but not slippery. They were almost running and Klimpt commanded them to go faster. Zorcia, flung over the first man's shoulder with her head dangling down, swung out as they dashed round a corner. Her head knocked on the wall and she moaned a little.

Steps led up to a door. All three men were breathing heavily. Klimpt motioned them to pause. He put up his hand for complete quiet and listened. From the far end of the corridor came the muffled sounds of shouting and struggle. On the outer side of the door was a sense of total silence. On the back of each man's neck, hairs rose.

From behind them, the sounds changed. Klimpt waved the men back a little, signalling that they were to go right on their exit. Starting at the bottom of the door, Klimpt shot back the bolts to pull it open. It shifted reluctantly on its stale oiled hinges and released a rush of warm air out into the night.

They ran out too, first Klimpt, then the man with Zorcia and lastly, the one carrying the chest.

Klimpt wanted to get to his car which was parked in another street parallel to this one. At the next turning they paused, leaning against the great wall of a bank, drawing breath and checking the street ahead.

Klimpt did not look back. In the wake of a stream of pulsing, noisy teen-filled cars, he ran forward, beckoning his men to follow as he headed for his car. The one with Zorcia also set off. The last man, who had been holding the chest, did not. He had fallen sprawling to the pavement and thrown the chest into the air as he released his hands to save himself.

Tucked into a recess in the wall of the bank, crouched Klara Schwartz, cloaked and quiet. As the man fell, the chest was flung towards her and Klara had a split second to protect herself before it landed, surprisingly lightly, in her lap. She pulled it and herself further into the shadows.

As Klimpt's man struggled to his knees, preparing to stand, two theatre doormen crept up to him, pushing him down to the ground again. One held his head, stifling his mouth as the other repeatedly kicked him. Then they ran off. Their hands were empty.

Klimpt reached his car. With all his attention on escape, he had only looked forward. He unlocked it, flinging open the doors for his men. The first shoved Zorcia into the back before sitting himself to drive. In alarm Klimpt glanced around for his second man. At first nothing, and then, from the direction of the night club, the sound of sirens.

Klimpt got into the car, ordering the driver to go. There was no thought of returning for the other man as they sped off, with the blue flashing light of a police car reflecting on the walls of the buildings just a little way behind them.

CHAPTER THIRTY-ONE

Pascal Explores The Light

The Mosaic household slept late the next morning, except for Pascal. The sun shone into the east windows, waking him as it beamed through a gap in the curtains of his bedroom and filled the bathroom next door with light. He climbed onto his toy chest, drew back the curtains and opened his window. Birdsong, mingled with distant church bells, caught his attention. He could smell the warmed lilac blossoms. He would go out.

On his bedroom floor were many things, including some silver holographic paper streamers left over from an astronaut's party some months ago. They caught the light and then his attention. He picked them up, waving them in the sun and watching the multiple reflections flickering on his walls and ceiling.

He took them to the bathroom and waved them more, dipping them into some water gathered in the bath from a dripping tap. Pascal became engrossed. As the sun continued to rise, an occasional crisp cloud passed across it. The angle of shadows and the quality of the light changed. Pascal ran more water into the bath and was then able to plunge the streamers deep into it, fascinated by the refraction and absorbed in making associations between all these wonders.

When Bruce shuffled into the bathroom, sleepy and crumpled, peeping at the day, there knelt his son, arms swooshing the water, head bent over intensely. Pascal looked up at his father with the joy of discovery in his eyes, telling him what he observed. Bruce heard it all, relishing the enthusiasm for life that his son was so willing to share, but he did not truly listen to the content. If he had, he might have realised that Pascal's thoughts were way beyond his years and that he was asking and addressing questions that he himself had never pondered.

CHAPTER THIRTY-TWO

Croft Silences His Garden

Mr Croft was mowing his lawn. As the weather was so pleasant, he had been to early communion, leaving himself a whole, clear day to get on with things. His neighbour on the left had tentatively asked him not to mow before eleven on a Sunday. He chose to ignore her half-baked request. He was a man with much to get done and as he had often observed, time and tide did indeed wait for no one.

Take Dorothy Windspill for example, he mused as he mowed past his rather splendid iris bed. Apart from pauses when she had her children, she had been at the county primary school for her entire teaching career. There she was still, just a class teacher - a fair enough one it had to be said, but still only a class teacher. She had never taken opportunities to progress her career. If she had played her cards right, gone for promotion, widened her experience in other schools, taken further study, she could be a head teacher by now, like him. Then, he thought with irritation, she wouldn't be around to hassle him in a way that felt similar to having his conscience pricked.

Mr Croft stopped the machine and took the grass clippings to the compost bin. It was a neat, green plastic one that he had bought by mail order. He had heard that too many clippings could sour the compost, but there, into the bin they could go, out of sight, tidy.

On his way back to the lawn, he bent to examine his petunias, newly hardened off and planted out only yesterday. That lower back pain nagged again, quite sharply in fact and he made a little gasp. When he refocused on his plants, he could not believe his eyes when he saw how much damage had been caused by slugs. Leaning forward like that, the surge of fury knotted in his stomach and he stared, enraged.

The soil was dried on top. At first he could see no sign of a slug. Then he found a snail. He took it and he took his gardening knife from his pocket, pulled out the blade and stabbed the snail, viciously twisting the knife. Then he turned on his heel, wincing as his back pain tugged again, and went to his garden shed. From a locked cupboard on a high shelf, he took down a packet of slug poison.

First, he stuffed about four of the pellets into the murdered snail. Then he threw it in the dustbin. He lavished more pellets on the remains of his petunias and for good measure, spread a liberal amount in many other places in his garden. He returned to his shed, locked up the poison and limped over to the hose to wash his hands. He leaned on the tap, a little breathless and rather worn out. Thrushes never sang to him.

CHAPTER THIRTY-THREE

Klara Begins Her Work

As he sat, pinned and winded by Klimpt's sharp manoeuvring of the table and of his exit, Mandrake stared ahead. His stare appeared blank but it was not. He saw the removal of two parts of his prize, where they had gone and, before the spasm of his diaphragm had passed, he had determined to follow. No one ever cheated him and he was not going to let that monster Klimpt get his hands on the girl. He wanted to save her.

The other players backed away from him. One hesitated, putting his hand towards the shambles of money still on the table. Mandrake saw this too and slammed his fist down onto the centre of the pile. There was no further dispute about that.

Standing up, Mandrake leaned over the table as his breathing returned to normal. He gathered the money, ordered it and put it inside his clothes. He was no longer the centre of attention, although a waiter passed him a glass of schnapps which he took. Then he made to follow Klimpt. He had to rescue that girl. He opened the side door and began to head down the corridor.

A hand grasped his belt and pulled him back. A huge man pushed past and completely blocked his way, standing with legs astride and hands on his hips. It was not only his body that created an effective block. His face said it all over again.

Mandrake shouted a protest, but he was restrained, his head grasped and thrust down towards his knees. On the floor, its edge caught beneath the bouncer's foot, lay a folded handkerchief. Mandrake grabbed it. As he was propelled back into the night club, the handkerchief was freed. Mandrake held it in his hand. As he shoved it into his pocket, he felt something small, flat and hard inside.

Mandrake was taken to the front door, the spy-hole opened and he was gestured to look through. Outside, there were two police cars. One of them whooped its siren. Two men dressed the same way as the one who had chased the girl, were disappearing up the far side of the street. Mandrake pulled back. He was pushed across the club, round the back of the bar, through the kitchen and out into the night.

He turned left and walked as fast as he could. The street was empty. He had a lot of money. However, he had also been cheated and more than that, the girl was now at the mercy of Klimpt. He needed to get away from the police and the chaos, but not without giving up on Klimpt. As he neared a junction with a vast bank on the corner, a stream of cars blaring music, hooting and waving with carefree people, sailed past him. Then he drew back as Klimpt, followed by a man carrying the girl, ran out from the other angle of the corner. The man who had taken the chest was no longer with them.

Mandrake watched them run down the street and turn off. He prepared to follow them but then, overwhelmingly, felt to draw back and stay out of view. He felt frightened. He felt that he was not alone in this and that another person nearby was also filled with fear. From around the corner he heard the sounds of muffled pain. He knew this sound so well. He had suffered to make it himself many times. His fear increased and he drew back even further until the awful sound stopped. Two doormen ran round the corner towards him, passed him and then vanished.

Mandrake stayed still. Then, a slight figure wearing a long cloak and carrying something, swiftly walked out from the corner. It headed towards a large park across the road junction and disappeared amongst the trees and bushes.

Mandrake stepped out of the shadows, ready to follow. Then a car from Klimpt's direction raced down the street towards him before careering away. Was he now alone? Listening for danger with the acuteness particular to those in great fear, Mandrake edged round the corner of the building. One of Klimpt's men lay there, beaten. He bent down to him as the flashing light of a police car came up from behind.

CHAPTER THIRTY-FOUR

A Fragile Peace

After breakfast, Bruce prepared to leave for High Table. Clive had stayed the night and he and Mary were still sipping tea.

"Is it over?" asked Mary. "Is it okay for us all to go back to normal?" Bruce stopped in his tracks, becoming pale.

"Why shouldn't it be?" he replied shortly. "It was Mandrake they were after, not us and he they have got, poor man." After that exchange, he became agitated and indecisive. He could not find his keys. He did not feel comfortable in his clothes and began to wonder if he should change them in some way. The collar of this shirt felt a little high, pressing into his neck just under his jaw. When he had found the keys and changed his shirt, he sat down again at the kitchen table.

"Well?" he began, "do we need to talk this over more?" Clive got up.

"I'll come with you," he said. Mary was taken aback.

"Yes. Of course," she said. "There's no reason to think they might come here, is there?" She kept further questions to herself in relation to the nervous approach home last night and her concern about this thing that Mandrake wanted and whether his kidnappers might want it too. Bruce and Clive smiled weakly. They also had thoughts that they did not want to share. Bruce kissed Mary absently and went out to the car.

"After all," Clive said quietly to Mary, "what happened, happened at High Table. I'm just giving him some sort of moral support as he goes back for the first time."

"Yes. Yes, of course," she replied, holding open the door for him and closing it gently as the men drove off.

Mary sat at the deserted table. She looked at its crumbs, spilt milk and blobs of jam. Pascal's place was distinctive. He spilt something of everything he ate. Then, whilst talking and forgetting to eat, he would rub bits of dropped food between his thumb and fingers, squish them onto different surfaces, seeming to examine their elasticity, their stickiness or perhaps their ability to remove one kind of dirt from his hands to replace it with another. Mary could only guess at these details, but she always knew where he had been sitting to eat. The dogs did too.

"I suppose this is a normal Sunday then," she sighed to the air.

She got up and began to clear the table, putting on the radio. For the moment, it was rock and roll. She danced as she tidied. Pascal and Jenny came in. Mary turned up the music and they all danced together, spontaneously creating a jam and honey pot clearing chain. They laughed at and with each other.

Jenny loved these moments when everyone was full of fun and happy. She took her mother's hand and twirled beneath it, gazing up at her with joy and hope. Perhaps today would be all right. Perhaps they would play together, a game of some sort, or dressing up even. She ran to the next room and grabbed a feathered hat from the dressing-up box. She had to be quick or the magic would go. When she leapt back into the kitchen, Mary laughed in delight, taking her hands as they twirled together. They circled their arms around Pascal, who danced between them for a moment before they resumed their table clearing.

"When the music finishes," thought Mary, "I'll have another go at getting Pascal to do that homework while he's in a cheerful mood." Immediately, in the midst of his wild and chaotic dancing, Pascal knocked his elbow on the back of a chair. He howled in pain, just as the music ended and the presenter began to talk. For talking, the radio was far too loud.

"Turn it down!" Mary shouted to Jenny, offending and disappointing her. Her lips quivered and tightened. Pascal wept. Mary felt angry. "It's too noisy!" she said, irritably leaving Pascal to turn down the sound herself. "Why do they have to talk such utter rubbish anyway? Who wants to know how much they drank last night or who's doing what, with who?" She turned to Pascal and kissed his elbow to take away the pain and she was also thinking of how much more difficult her day had just become. Jenny was crestfallen.

Mary took Pascal onto her lap. She stroked his head and kissed the back of his neck where his soft hair nestled in the dip of two tendons. She held out her hand to Jenny who came over. They put their arms round each other and stayed like this a while. All the time, Mary's thoughts were splashed with her anxiety as to how to get harmony and homework into the house at the same time.

"Well," she said, "what shall we do today?"

CHAPTER THIRTY-FIVE

A Reunion For Mandrake

Mandrake could hear Bob Hodges and the nurse talking close by. He couldn't hear the words. His mind was out of focus, pulled out of shape by the sadness deep inside him and the relentless craving of his body, but he could hear distress and it aroused his own all the more. A new noise began to vibrate in his head. He was moaning. The voices stopped and someone approached him. He tensed, anticipating disturbance, but it did not come.

He felt a touch. His feet were being held firmly. The touch was gentle and did not unsettle him and he was glad of it. His grandmother Gwendolyne came to his mind, as a flood of benevolence began to wash through him. At the same moment, he felt and yet longed for her presence. He drifted upwards and was able to look down into the room. A nurse was holding his feet, her eyes closed. All around her there was light. He could see it flowing through her hands and into him. The man in the next bed was sitting back against his pillows. He also had light around him but it was not so bright.

Then from this place, Mandrake turned away, his vision filling with a rich, blue light and at its centre, glorious white. He was filled with joy and moved towards the light, feeling his own transformation. He welcomed this completely. He did not look back.

Gwendolyne was there before him. She was smiling at him, radiant. She did not put out her arms for him as she had when he was a child. Instead, she held up one hand, palm facing him, an unmistakable sign for him to stop.

Even without her touch, Mandrake was enfolded in her love and acceptance - a return to a place long denied him in life. He moved closer to her and the coloured lights that seemed to flow from and all around her. He wanted those lights to shine on him, but her hand said no. She gestured that he was to turn around.

"Robin, you can go back to life and find your family. You have greater choices to make than this." He longed for her to hold him. He put out his arms and she embraced him. The strength that he had lost began to trickle back. In this way, they stayed together for an unknowable time as the trickle became a flood, filling the places within that had felt so empty, so lonely.

When they let each other go, he felt able to return. Moving away, keeping his grandmother in his sights for as long as he could, Mandrake found himself once again looking down on the ward. Nothing had changed. The nurse still held his feet. The man next to him still reclined in his bed. Then Mandrake was back in his body, with its painful and endangered life. But now something had changed. In the centre of his pain, he felt a sensation so long absent, that it took thought to identify it. Then he recognised what it was. It was hope.

CHAPTER THIRTY-SIX

Bruce's Property Is Damaged

The previous evening when Bruce had left High Table man-handled by Mandrake, he had not set the burglar alarm. When he and Clive arrived on Sunday morning, Gemma was standing out on the pavement. The plate glass window on the right of the door was smashed. Gemma ran forward and leaned into the car as Clive rolled down the window.

"I've just got here! I've called the police, but I knew you'd soon be here so I didn't call you. Mary doesn't know." Her face was full of anxiety and concern. "They should be here soon. I've touched nothing. I don't know. I really don't know. What are things coming to?" Bruce took her arm as he got out of the car. Gemma helped him to regain his balance as he tripped on the dangling loop of his seat belt. He cursed and then thanked her.

The door was broken too, with wood splintered and glass shattered. It crunched beneath his feet. The sun shone over the scattered shards, throwing up tiny prisms of light which danced along the bright paintwork. Bruce noticed them but they did not touch him. He turned to Clive.

"What's going on?" he asked, turning his gaze to the ground.

"It's probably just coincidence, you know, not connected," said Clive. Bruce looked up slowly, right into Clive's eyes. As he began to tremble, the police arrived. He had not heard the siren as they approached. Now its sudden and deafening noise confused and frightened him. If the kidnappers hadn't found what they were looking for on Mandrake, and they hadn't found it here, then they'd be heading for Stonelea.

He ran to the car, gesturing crazily at the policemen inside. They opened the window, anticipating behaviour within the normal range of distress and outrage that burglary kindles in its victims. This was different.

"My wife!" Bruce yelled. "My wife and children! Quick, come with me." He tried to get into the back of the car but the doors were locked. The delay caused by questions from the police drove Bruce to distraction. He could barely articulate enough to explain. The police were aware of Mandrake's abduction, noted in the shift handover that morning. Backed by Clive, Bruce made his fears known. Calling through for support, the officer let the men into the car and set off swiftly. Gemma, left on the pavement and now at the centre of a small crowd, put her hands on her hips and gazed after the car as it pulled away.

CHAPTER THIRTY-SEVEN
The Worries of Herr Schwartz

The proprietor of Wien Nachts had an unruly daughter. Herr Schwartz had tried his best to bring up Klara correctly, yet the environment of his night club provided such a contradiction to all that he told her she ought to do, that it was hard to maintain the discipline he sought. On the night of the extraordinary events connected with Herr Klimpt and that waif of a girl, his daughter also disappeared.

As a little girl, Klara had often vanished for minutes at a time when, conventional wisdom held, she was far too young to do so safely. Then it had been for hours and more recently, for days. On each occasion, no amount of reproach had persuaded her to change her ways. When she did not return this time, Herr Schwartz did nothing but wait and fret, as usual.

She was only seventeen years old, although he acknowledged to himself that she was beyond her years in many ways. He hoped that her natural luck and wits would provide for her but then, when he thought of the size of the world and all that went on in it, he also believed in her vulnerability. His wife said that Klara would be all right. She said that she missed her too, wanting to know about and share her life, although the sadness she felt was connected to her own sense of loss and had nothing to do with Klara. Klara was a brilliant companion, but a hair-raising daughter to bring up. She wanted her home again for sure. However, she could not in all the world see Klara as vulnerable. The idea made her smile.

"Just think of the vulnerability of the world, my darling husband. Just think of that," and he would smile and try to do it.

CHAPTER THIRTY-EIGHT

Klara's Good Intentions

On the night she disappeared, Klara had been at Wien Nachts. She was supposed to stay upstairs in the house. Her rooms were high up in the building. Her willingness to conform had passed away even more swiftly than her childhood. She came down when she wanted, hanging around behind the scenes, always with a good view of the goings-on in the club.

On this night she saw Klimpt playing. She knew him. He disgusted her. He was not as ancient as her father, but at his age he should have known that he could not be in the least attractive to her. He came too close whenever they had an encounter. It could be the briefest of meetings, a passing by, a catching of eye. Yet whatever the occasion he would imply his sexual attraction to her, inviting her to engage with him without deference. His presumption made him all the more repulsive.

He was gambling with other men. They were all old except for the dark haired Englishman. He seemed so sensitive and sad. She wanted him to win. She wanted him to have all the money.

When the Englishman won, the unexpected happened. The unexpected enlivened Klara. Klimpt surprised her by leaving the money and taking his men to one of the side rooms. When they emerged with the girl and her box, making for the underground corridor, Klara knew where they would make their exit onto the street. She decided to get that box for the Englishman.

She put on her cloak and ran through the kitchens, turning left alongside the buildings and crouched in the shadows of the entrance to the bank around the corner. She guessed that Klimpt would come this way, avoiding the front of the club and its possible crowds. She didn't know what she would do when they came past. Perhaps she would follow them.

They were almost beside her when they paused to avoid a crowd of kids driving by. It was then that the last man fell and fate hurled the box at her. She put up her arms to protect herself and caught it in her lap. It seemed almost weightless. Then instinctively, she pulled herself and it even further into the hollow of the door, as two doormen from the Theatre Wagner fell upon Klimpt's man, beating him savagely before running off.

Klara could see the lights of the police cars as they drew in. She left the man to their tender care and ran across the road to the park.

CHAPTER THIRTY-NINE

Klara Begins to Melt Away

It was Klara's intention to somehow give the box back to the Englishman. When she reached the park, she hid amongst the bushes. From there, she saw him creep round the corner of the bank and stop beside the beaten man. Before he could do anything, the police were upon him and they summoned an ambulance and arrested the Englishman.

As for herself, Klara was sure that she had not been seen. She felt exhilarated by what had happened to her, although sickened by the violence that she had witnessed. Why had those people been chasing the girl anyway? Was it for her or for the chest? If it was the latter, there could be someone creeping up on her right now.

Klara looked about the park. The street lights caused the trees and bushes to cast a shadow all along one edge. If she ran across a short clearing, she could get all the way to Elsa's house in the dark. Her chances of being unseen were good. She could go round the back into their little garden. She would stay there and avoid any risk of attention at home. Then she would plan her next step.

There was an understanding with Elsa's family that Klara and she could come and go to each other's homes as they liked. The two girls had grown up together and were as close as sisters. Klara stole round the side of Elsa's house and sped up the steps towards some french windows which opened onto a balcony. Taking the key from a cranny below the window sill, she unlocked the doors and went into the house.

"About turn!" said Elsa's father breathlessly out of the dark of the drawing room that she had just entered. Klara was on her way to the light switch. She could see nothing, but of course, she recognised Larse's voice. It was the one he had always used to command the two girls. For Elsa's sake, Klara usually obeyed and so by habit, she turned to face the french windows again.

Although it was dark she could just make out two figures moving, reflected in the glass. Larse was standing up, putting on his jacket. The other figure lying on the sofa sat up. The rustle of clothes being adjusted, subsided, finishing with the sound of a zip being pulled. Klara had intruded on a love-making session. She burned with curiosity as to who the woman could be and began to turn.

"Wait!" said Larse. "This way now." He crossed the room, opening a door onto the hallway. A dim light shone there and by this light, he gestured Klara to leave. The temptation to look back was great. She resisted it. She was curious, but not to the degree that she wanted to risk Larse's temper.

"Hullo Klara. Good bye!" came the amused voice of Elsa's mother, as Klara walked out into the hallway. So that was all. Klara felt a mixture of relief and disappointment and also, she realised, surprise.

Larse came out with her and shut the door quietly behind him, leaning back against it and keeping his hold on the door handle. He looked down at her.

"What have you there?" he asked, nodding at the bulk beneath her cloak.

"A prize!" she replied. "Sorry to disturb you," she added, turning to go upstairs to Elsa's room. She swung her hips a little as she went, pretending to herself that this was just what happened when she mounted steps.

CHAPTER FORTY

More Of Bruce's Property Is Damaged

After Pascal hurt his elbow, Mary asked him and Jenny to choose what they wanted to do that day. Pascal wanted to take the dogs down to the river. Jenny wanted to watch television. This felt like a much needed gift.

"Okay," said Mary, "we'll take the dogs out later. Meanwhile Jenny, you can watch telly and Pascal, you can get that school work finished." Pascal was still on her lap. She felt him tense with resistance. Her own body reflected this tension. Jenny moved away towards the television, putting out her hand to turn it on.

"Just a minute!" Mary said urgently. "Let Pascal and me go on up first." She got up, keeping hold of his hand. As his feet touched the floor, he crumpled down into a heap of passive resistance. "Come on darling," she said. "Up we go!" She tugged a little at his arm, but he remained completely limp.

Mary felt sick. Here she was yet again, facing the same situation all alone. Just now, there were programmes on the television that Jenny would enjoy and hence leave her free to attend to Pascal. However, if Pascal continued with this behaviour, the programmes would become less attractive and then she would be torn between the needs of both children. In the state he was now, Pascal was pretty well immovable.

Mary began to slide him over the kitchen floor. She thought that if at least she could get him out into the hallway, Jenny could have the television on. It could only be a matter of moments before Jenny's patience would wear out and she would turn it on anyway. Then she would have conflict with both children.

When Mary got Pascal to the doorway, she began to roll him over the threshold. She anticipated the relief that she would feel to get him through and to shut the door. Her heart beat faster and the adrenaline quickened too. Then Pascal went rigid, jamming his feet and shoulders into the architrave. Jenny turned on the television and it was Sesame Street - a favourite of Pascal's.

"I'm not going upstairs!" he shouted, catching Mary off guard. In that split second, he crawled past her legs to the television. He sat on the floor, wrapping himself intractably around a leg of the kitchen table. Outraged, Mary strode theatrically across the room and pulled out the plug. Fury erupted from both children at once.

"You always spoil everything!" Jenny shouted.

"I'm not doing that stupid writing!" yelled Pascal. "We hate you!"

"Don't you dare speak to me like that!" Mary yelled back. She was on their side, but the world had made her alien to them. Why couldn't they see that? It hurt so much to be apart from her children in this way. She had given of every resource she had to convey her love to them. This sense of separation blasted her with failure. She felt frightened and angry. "Don't you dare! Now! Pascal! Upstairs!" She slapped his back. She wanted to slap his head. She wanted to kick him for the distress that he brought. She was overwhelmed with horrible feelings, spilling out of control, all around her home and all over her adored children. She stamped her foot.

"Get up!" she cried, beginning to prise Pascal's fingers away from the table leg. Jenny was trying to put the plug back into the socket. "Leave that! You're making it worse. Just wait, wait!" She marched across the room, self-righteous and fearful, her hand raised. Jenny cowed. She was frightened too. She was frightened of her mother and she was frightened of her own feelings.

Mary went to the draining board where the washing up was waiting. She picked out a bowl and threw it to the floor. As it crashed down, china sprayed out in all directions. She continued to shout at Pascal and Jenny who cried in bewilderment and frustration. As she raised a dinner plate and threw it down, Jenny noticed a police car and then another pull into the driveway. Three policemen, Daddy and Clive came running towards the house.

From the outside, it sounded as if hell had been let loose. In a way, this was true. It was the sound of a mother, snapping.

CHAPTER FORTY-ONE

Bruce Sees An Incomprehensible Sight

Through the door, Bruce could hear Mary shouting and the children crying. Something was being smashed up. He should be in there, between his family and this fiend. He should never have left them.

"They're here! Help me Clive!" he urged, as he fumbled for his key. The police officer held Bruce back.

"Let's take it slowly," said Sergeant Palmer. He was thinking that this might turn out to be a hostage situation although, from his experience through twenty-three years of policing, these noises had more of the flavour of a domestic. Still, in the light of the abduction that Mr Mosaic had reported last night and the break-in at his restaurant, he couldn't afford to take any chances. Palmer took the key from Bruce's desperate hand and softly unlocked the door.

The dogs were barking and jumping at the door. When he opened it, they rushed out. They were upset and agitated, quietening at Bruce's presence and then running off to investigate the police car.

Down the hallway came the sound of more china breaking. Bruce could hear Jenny and Mary shouting. Pascal was wailing. Palmer, confident now that this was family stuff, gestured for Bruce to go to the kitchen. He opened the door quickly, just as Mary threw down another plate. It crashed into the fragments already on the floor and shot across the vinyl to his feet. Bruce's mouth dropped open. He could not understand the sight. Neither could he recognise the woman who stood before him.

Pascal sat under the table with china debris scattered around him. He was curled into a ball, too alarmed even to rock. Jenny stood apart, her face tear stained. Clive knelt beside her, letting her bury her face in the comfort of his shoulder.

"I think we'd better be getting back to your restaurant sir," Palmer said to Bruce. "Perhaps you could join us as soon as possible?" He turned and left.

"Well," said Clive, as Jenny drew away from him, "I'll be going along now. I'll phone later," and he left too.

CHAPTER FORTY-TWO

Klimpt Begins To Steal From Zorcia

How the police had come to be alerted, Klimpt did not know. It was not usual in these situations. He had forgone the money and now he had lost the chest. All that he had left was the girl. This certainly gave focus to his lust. He decided that nothing was going to spoil his enjoyment of her. He had experienced many times how power and money attracted women, but those types were simply that, types. This one was different. Artless and in her current doped state, she would be unable to stop him.

Directing his driver to head for Ybbs where his boat was moored, Klimpt put up the glass screen between them, pulled down the blinds and settled himself to relish the journey. By the time they reached Ybbs, Klimpt was satisfied and Zorcia was awake.

CHAPTER FORTY-THREE

Extraordinary Objects

Klara had always been blessed with good fortune. Now, late at night, she possessed a desirable object and no one apart from Mandrake, whose arrest she had witnessed, had seen her take it. She did not know that for those who sought the chest, the trail had gone cold, leaving only a tenuous interest in Mandrake. That night, she shoved the chest under Elsa's bed, pulled out the arm of the bedroom sofa and settled down to sleep under her usual blanket.

In the morning, Elsa woke up to find Klara in her room. She was snoring a little as her head had dropped back, resting on a pile of clothes. Elsa looked at her with affection, wondering anew how she managed to make the world go her way with such relaxed success. She was mostly good to be with except that sometimes she was a bit like a cat. She was so independent that occasionally Elsa was hurt by Klara's readiness to live with or without her, as if it made no difference to her at all. Free-spirited and feline she might be, yet deep down, Elsa did not doubt Klara's loyalty to their friendship.

Elsa read a magazine until Klara awoke and told her about the night before, bidding her to look under her own bed for the evidence. They pulled it out.

"What's inside?" asked Elsa.

"I have no idea," Klara answered. "All I know is that it stirred up a lot of interest last night. It may have been just the girl that they were after, but I prefer to believe that this is worth something."

"Are you going to open it?"

"Of course!" beamed Klara. She was used to picking locks although this was different from any she had tried before. There was no keyhole. She took the padlock in her hands, looking and feeling carefully for its secret. As she searched with her fingertips, alert to the slightest movement within the lock, she reflected on the strangeness of the events that had brought her to this moment; the uniqueness of the chest itself and how it had come to her, falling so lightly into her lap and yet weighing heavy in her hands as she had run to hide. She was intrigued and grateful, desiring to understand. The lock sprung open.

"How did you do that?" exclaimed Elsa. Klara looked up.

"I'm not sure."

She lifted the lid. Her curiosity burned. A smell of stale air began to drift as she opened the chest. Elsa leaned forward. Light streamed in through the tall bedroom windows. Inside the chest, some sort of brown animal hair formed an obscuring layer. It hinted that it would stink when disturbed. Elsa didn't want to touch it.

"Open a window. We're going to need some air," said Klara. Elsa went to the window, opening it to the still morning and admitting the sounds of a spacious city beginning its day. "Let's spread this newspaper out on the floor so that I've got somewhere to put this stuff." When Klara touched the hair, it was dry and brittle. It did not smell as much as they had anticipated although the dust rose readily, tickling their eyes and noses. Klara put some aside. Dense, powdered fragments fell from her hands as she moved it. She parted the hair further and found a long, clay jar. It was sealed at one end.

"My God! A genie!" said Elsa. "Don't open it!" At first she laughed. Then she became serious. "Really Klara. Please don't open it. It could be something weird."

"Let's see if there's anything else," said Klara. She took out more hair. The deeper she went, the more dust there was. There were no more jars, but built into a corner at the bottom of the chest was a small drawer compartment. Klara gestured to Elsa that she should be the one to open it, but she declined. Klara reached down and tugged at the little wooden handle. The drawer slid open and she pulled it right out, putting it on the floor between them. The sun shone onto the carpet and into the drawer where there lay four little packages, wrapped in parchment. Like the hair, the parchment was brittle. It would not unfold without threatening to crack and break.

"What shall we do? We shouldn't damage something so ancient. It may be unique," said Elsa.

"Let's choose just one to open. Whatever we decide to do next, it will leave three undisturbed. Which one?" Klara placed them in a row before her. "How about this one?"

"Okay," Elsa said reluctantly. Klara broke off a folded end as she tried to prise open the little package. She pulled out something hard, cool and transparent. The sun reflected from it with brilliance. It was not a jewel. It was a lens.

"Well," said Elsa, "I don't know what to think. Giant jewels, embroidered cloth, a crown or some golden coins would have more appeal to me."

"Me too," said Klara distractedly. She felt deeply touched by these things and did not mean what she said. As she held them, she experienced a peace which expanded from deep within her, making her feel different.

Sitting in a pool of sunlight, she put the lens to her right eye. Cascades of blues filled her vision, sparkling and swirling from the edges of her sight. Her ears hummed and her heart lifted. The word 'glorious' came repeatedly to her mind.

"What are you going to do with this stuff?" Elsa's question cut through Klara's absorption.

"I'm sure it's benevolent stuff. It needs looking after carefully." Elsa did a double-take at such an uncharacteristic statement from her friend. "Look through this lens, Elsa." Warily, she took it and held it to her eye. She was sitting in the shade. When she looked, velvet darkness fell before her. All was silent, at peace. Then in the distance, pinpricks of light appeared, bringing with them a hint of roses to her tongue. Klara waited. When Elsa took the lens away from her eye, they shared what they had seen and sensed.

Later, leaving the chest in a corner of Elsa's huge wardrobe, Klara carefully packed her strange new treasures into her rucksack between the folds of her clothes. She was going to Milan. Her friend Pietze worked there in the science faculty at the university.

Klara, appearing to be a student traveller, left Vienna later that day. She attracted no attention, moving freely out of the ring that had been closing in on the contents of the chest.

CHAPTER FORTY-FOUR
Destructive Plundering

As Klara was making her way to Milan, Klimpt held Zorcia on his boat, going up the Danube to Linz. Zorcia had no idea where she was. She did not know how much time had passed since she had run into the night club and been drugged and virtually sold. She was cold and frightened and she had lost her precious token of true love - the handkerchief from Clive. She had used it to wrap the key to the trunk after opening it to remove the chest. Now it was gone and without it, she felt as weak as the feint colours woven into the flimsy curtains of the cabin. When she thought of the tiny pricks of light that were all that could be seen of the vastness of the stars, she felt convinced of her own insignificance. Klimpt had shut her up in a cabin while he and another man were getting the boat under way. She vaguely remembered being pushed in there hours ago.

She felt and indeed she was, dirty. There was no water in the cabin and nothing else with which to clean herself. She knew what had been done to her. It had bruised her and made her smell. She could feel Klimpt's semen making her damp and repulsive to herself. She thought that she was probably very hungry but that food, if offered, would stick in her throat.

After the boat was well under way, Klimpt came down to Zorcia. He brought her some food; bread, smoked ham, cheese and coffce. The diesel fumes drifting back, the strong smells of the food and the sight of Klimpt made her nauseated. When she refused it, he locked the door behind him and came towards her. He pinned her against the cabin wall with his forearms across her chest. His strength, his disregard for her and his need to bully others to submission, made it impossible for Zorcia to stop him and enabled Klimpt to do whatever he wanted.

140

CHAPTER FORTY-FIVE
Mandrake's Fruitless Pursuit

A fter his arrest, Mandrake had left Austria within twenty-four hours. Deprived of his winnings and the opportunity to rescue the girl, he had returned to Stonelea which he had bought some years before during a winning streak.

On the flight home in the aeroplane toilet, Mandrake at last had a private moment in which to unfold the handkerchief that he had snatched from beneath the bouncer's foot. Inside was a key. Perhaps it was for the chest. It looked quite ordinary, but it had come from the girl. He had seen the handkerchief falling from her pocket when she was being carried off. When he got home he put the key on a chain and wore it around his neck, always.

The handkerchief was quite small. It was white with a woven pattern round the edges and was grubby. In one corner, written in what looked like biro, were the letters C and Z enclosed in a heart. Mandrake assumed that this was important to the girl. Was she C or Z, or neither? He kept it in his possession. The idea that he would one day return it and use the key never left him, but it became overlaid with the distractions of a different addiction because during these intervening years, Mandrake succumbed to heroin.

The death at Stonelea of a friend who overdosed one humid, mid-summer night, heralded the end of an era for Mandrake. It pushed him into taking the action that he had so long abandoned. He sold his house and headed for Austria, thinking that in some way he might pick up the trail.

His return journey to Vienna was difficult, dictated by his need for heroin. He headed for Amsterdam. He knew how to make contacts and move along a network of suppliers. His addiction drove him to take on a courier role as he moved across the continent.

When his supply was assured, he could focus on his journey. The route was defined by his delivery points and he made progress well enough. He stayed in horrible places. He knew that each person he met was almost certainly as desperate as he. Everywhere had bad vibes; they were part of the buildings and part of the people. Mandrake was used to this. He had lived with this undercurrent of desperation ever since his grandmother had been murdered.

When he arrived in Vienna, he delivered his package and received payment. This would see him through for a while and he felt some sort of security, knowing where to go when he needed to replenish his supply. He made his way to Wien Nachts. Although the streets had changed a little, it was not difficult to recall the way. Mandrake had intelligence and good memory to aid him, despite the interference caused by his addiction.

Mandrake knew that he would be unable to get into the club. He was too dishevelled now. He walked up and down the street trying to decide what he would actually do now that he was here.

Walking round to the back door where he had been thrown out all those years ago just before his arrest, he found the door open. Sounds and smells of cooking and washing-up came out, whilst in the doorway leaned a sous-chef, wearing the international costume of chequered trousers, white apron and hat. He was taking a break, smoking a cigarette and watching the world go by. As Mandrake approached, the two men exchanged a glance that hinted of recognition. Mandrake had the advantage of context. The sous-chef could not immediately place this depleted man. Mandrake stopped and tried to focus his eyes upon him.

"Do you speak English?"

"A little. I know you?"

"You were here six years ago? I came here to gamble one night. There was a girl and trouble. The police were called."

"Yes. This night I remember," said the sous-chef. "How bad you look." Mandrake balked at this candid observation.

"I'm back," he said. "I won the chest and I won the girl. I want to find them." He fumbled at the neck of his shirt, clumsily pulling the key out on its chain. "See this? It's all I've got left. All I've got to go on." He tucked it back in.

"That was far in the past," said the sous-chef.

"Yes. What has happened since?" The sous-chef looked at Mandrake again. He had not liked the gamble. Even more, he had never liked Klimpt and particularly not the cheating.

"This thing to you I tell. Not only you that night disappeared. The daughter Klara, since such time she has not been seen. She has gone other times but this time is a long time. Klimpt comes but no more such gambling. Klimpt is a man with whatever he wants, he can get. People like you he uses, I think." He threw his cigarette to the ground and trod it out. "Now again I work. Good bye. Good chances." He went back to the kitchen, leaving Mandrake alone.

CHAPTER FORTY-SIX

The Plans Of Blanche

In the time that had elapsed between the disappearance of the chest and Mandrake's return to Vienna, Wien Nachts had been watched. So had Mandrake. Both were just two of the means by which Blanche intended to trace the chest that had so nearly come into her hands. Now that he was back, she hoped that he would provide some sort of new lead.

She had almost dismissed him as being of no further interest, especially after he had declined into drug addiction. However, there was something beneath his apparent weakness that led her to keep an eye on him. His return to Vienna might herald change for them both.

Klimpt, she had dismissed. On her stage, he was small-fry. He had taken the girl and she was now down at the bottom of hope, somewhere in Salzburg. Klimpt had his power, but he moved in a different league to her. He chased power of the type that uses money as a currency. Blanche could never be satisfied with stopping at that level. For her, money was secondary to the power that she sought - power over the hearts and minds of people.

Blanche did not consider herself to belong to any one nation although she had been born and raised in Switzerland. She moved around the globe in a nationhood of controllers who operated networks across the planet, supporting and developing the chains that put thinking into bondage; usury, red tape, the pursuit of glamour, excitement or convention, media ownership and the suppression of information - these were just some of the means by which people were disempowered and enslaved.

Occasionally, certain things would come to light that must be kept out of circulation because they had the potential to challenge narrow, complacent thinking. Religious fundamentalism and scientific fundamentalism for example, helped to keep people's minds stagnant, whilst creating an illusion of true exploration. Knowledge was power and Blanche knew that she was ruthless enough to kill in order to contain it. Knowing of its rumoured origins, the chest would almost certainly throw doubt on to currently accepted thinking, certainly in the field of science and possibly in the realms of religious thought too.

Blanche did not like to see literacy and numeracy programmes. With the ability to access written information and to be able to calculate, let alone use mathematics as a tool for exploring the abstract, it was much more difficult to enslave people and their minds. These skills liberated and empowered people. It made them less malleable. It therefore followed that as access to education was becoming more widespread, so certain types of information should be withheld. Now there was the internet, beyond the control of governments and individuals. People could send and receive information that had previously been suppressed or at least inaccessible. These times were challenging for her. To sustain enslavement, the masters have to be convincing.

Blanche did not understand quite how it worked, but it was having an effect in some quarters and seemed to be strengthening. It was the growing interest in 'spirituality'. Religion was one thing. Dogma, fear and conditioning were immensely useful controlling methods, but there was a lot of talk and literature about at the moment regarding spiritual awakening, having a relationship with the self, or what some described as 'the God within'. Personal responsibility was another buzz-word. Blanche recognised the liberating potential of a world where people stopped blaming.

At fifteen, Blanche had taken an autumn walk with her grandfather. He had pointed to the top of a tall hedge. The late afternoon sun, slanting along the ridge of the hill beyond and spilling across the meadows, made brilliant the red of a spray of rosehips. They dangled above her head, nodding to the rhythm of the wind.

"When I see something as simple yet as beautiful as that, my heart sings," said her grandfather. "All that I have lived through, what I have seen happen on this continent in my lifetime, what I know to be happening in the world now, is kept in proportion by the promise contained within such a sight." He turned to Blanche. "Whatever happens in your life, never give up. The natural spirit of joy that is within all life is there to aid you, to help you to overcome all obstacles to happiness. No one can take that away from you - once you have understood it!"

He was holding Blanche by the shoulders, looking into her eyes with such hope for her future. She stared at him with cold interest. Perhaps what he had told her could be useful after all if she turned it around. This talk of the human spirit - did many people believe in it and if so, could she use this belief? Or did it actually exist, in which case how might this knowledge serve her?

She had since observed that this inconvenient spark within people could be suppressed by distraction. Poverty was a good distraction and so was greed, false hope, dogma, hurry and ambition. Keeping them too busy to think, kept the machine of delusion well oiled.

Although she had good contacts among drug dealers, keeping track of Mandrake was not easy. He had to be secretive on his own account and had his own methods for keeping out of trouble. When he disappeared for three days in Vienna, Blanche feared that he had slipped through her net and that he might possibly be on to something. In fact, he was stoned in an empty flat belonging to the elderly parents of the sous-chef. They had gone away for a short holiday and Mandrake had been let in by their son.

When Blanche heard that he had been seen again, she set up a permanent tail. Vic began to follow Mandrake. As soon as he was aware that he was being tailed, Mandrake became fearful. He had no certain idea why this man should be following him. It made it difficult for him to score. It was so difficult that he had to drop the idea of finding Zorcia, or making any attempt to recover his chest. He focussed entirely on finding ways to get his next fix without being stopped.

As soon as he could, he arranged another courier job and

began to head back to England, looking over his shoulder constantly. He thought that he had shaken off his pursuer. Then, on the cross channel ferry, he was sure that he was under surveillance again, this time from a different man.

It was true. Dave had taken over from Vic in an attempt to catch Mandrake off-guard. By the time they got to Ramsgate, they were both following him. Blanche had told them to find out what Mandrake knew. At first they had hoped that he would lead them somewhere, but as Mandrake continued his journey with his constant requirements for more heroin, it seemed that he was simply going where his courier work took him.

Back in England, although it seemed likely that he was heading for his home town, Dave and Vic knew that he had sold his house, so they could not be sure where he would go. They continued to watch him in case he veered off and they could discover more. By the time he reached Salisbury, it was obvious that he was home for home's sake. Blanche instructed them to seize him.

When Mandrake understood that the chase had changed from follow to catch, he tried to find a means of escape. He knew that High Table was near-by. It was a place he sometimes went and he had the added link that he had sold Stonelea to the proprietor.

There was also one other thing. It was about Mary Mosaic. She was his sister. This was something he had kept to himself but it somehow made High Table into a safe house, didn't it? When he got to the restaurant, it was closing and the car that was pursuing him was not far behind. He hammered on the door to be let in. It was the fear of what might happen next that made Mandrake resort to threats. It was the way people got what they wanted, he'd noticed.

CHAPTER FORTY-SEVEN

Zorcia Escapes

Klimpt continued to rape Zorcia as often as he wished. Only occasionally did he go up on deck to check his man. By the time they reached Linz, he had had enough of her. Her crying had become an unattractive nuisance. He left her locked in a cabin and went out.

While he was gone, his man took a basin of water, soap and a rough towel to Zorcia. She was in a pitiful state and his barricaded heart was almost touched at the sight of her. He turned quickly and left.

Zorcia did not recognise herself in this suddenly very old, hurt and tired person. As she washed, grateful for the comfort of the water, tender from Klimpt's cruelty, she gazed out of the dirty window. She could see only boats, thick, litter-strewn water, stained concrete jetties and beyond them, huge buildings. She could see nothing green or growing apart from dark slime at the water's edge.

"My heart has stopped singing," she thought. Her throat tightened and she felt empty. She put her hand in her pocket for the handkerchief that Clive had given her and was reminded that even that had gone. "This is not me," she said aloud. "I am somewhere else." It was at this moment that she began to exist beyond her body, placing her care and joy into the shining ball that had shifted from around her whole being, to a place just above her head, slightly to the left.

Klimpt returned, took Zorcia out of the cabin and put her off the boat. He cruised away. She found her way to Saltzburg. If she had known that there was a Yugoslav community there, she might have sought them out. But she found a way to survive, learned enough German to negotiate her deals and by the time she discovered its existence, she was too ashamed to make herself known.

Sometimes, in the summer, she would take herself to the Untersburg Mountain outside Salzburg and lie beneath the trees. Beneath her, she had heard, the Emperor Charlemagne slept, waiting to be called as his beard grew long. She waited to be called too. If he could lie there sleeping all these years, then so could she. Her mind would turn to her home village and what had happened there. She would think of her family, her community, her lover and her choice to leave with Stojanka. What had become of them all?

Schnapps made it easy to become sentimental. Tears of sweetness, joy and sorrow would run from her eyes. Surely something would happen to change her life and she could begin to reel in that shining part of her, and live.

CHAPTER FORTY-EIGHT

Keeping The Pieces

It was so good to see Pietze again. Klara surprised him in his flat. He helped her to heave her luggage up the narrow stairway with its terracotta paint and through the bright blue door at the top. He was talking with a friend in his kitchen. Dusk had fallen and they had lit candles which poured a warm and gentle light into the room. Outside, trees danced at the windows. They were drinking wine and eating biscuits. Klara was greeted with the warmth that Pietze had learned from the Italians. He hugged, fed and included her.

Later, when they were alone, Klara told him about the chest and its contents. He was intensely interested as Klara took them out of her rucksack and put them on the table. When she held them, the same sense of peace that she had felt before, enveloped her again. She watched Pietze as he began to handle them for the first time. She heard him give a short gasp. He turned to her.

"Before I even study these, I know they are special. I can feel it here," he said, as he touched the centre of his chest. He took the opened lens from its cover.

"Hold it to your eye," said Klara. He did so, walking over to the window and gazing up into the sky at the first evening star struggling to penetrate the light pollution of a busy city. He was so dazzled by the light coming through that he snatched the lens from his eye to check the direction of his gaze, relocated the star and looked once more. He was dazzled again.

"What is it?" asked Klara. "What do you see?"

"It's too bright. Don't try. I was just looking up at that star" he said, pointing. "In all my years in science I have never seen anything like this." He held the lens over his hand. "Look here," he said, holding his hand out to Klara.

"Look at how much it magnifies my skin." Klara leaned over to look. Although the candlelight was pale, she could see the magnification. As she continued to look, Pietze's skin seemed to change beneath the lens. Every skin-tone formed itself in to beautiful, tessellating shapes, the colours swirling in subtle contrast to each other.

"What do you see, Pietze?"

"I see myself as never before," he replied. Klara told him what she and Elsa had experienced.

"The wrapping suggests that this object is truly ancient. If it is, it is going to throw some currently accepted science history into great confusion - if anyone out there is willing to think carefully enough to get to that point."

"Don't be half-hearted Pietze. Come on, the answer may be in the jar. Or do we need to take these things to an expert?" asked Klara.

"Let us be our own experts. If we take this elsewhere, we'll probably never get to see or touch them again, let alone know about them. They could disappear into a vault, leaving the world no wiser than now.

"After what you told me about the interest shown in the chest, it might be wiser to keep this to ourselves until we know what we've got. There are some extraordinary people about who collect these things for selfish ends. We'll be careful, but let's stay in charge.

"I've seen it happen, Klara. Some new piece of information tries to come to light but then some people do all they can to suppress it because it doesn't serve their interests. Think of what we have here already - a strange, heavy yet weightless chest with a mysterious lock, to say nothing of the way it came to you, this remarkable lens and so far this is all we've looked at. People should get to see and know about such things. We can't risk handing it over to someone else."

Pietze was standing, leaning forward over the kitchen table. The candles flickered, casting their glow on his face and arms. He cupped the lens in one hand, covering it with the other. Then Klara said,

"I'm all for keeping it out of rogue hands, but let's just think about this. Whatever is in the jar could get damaged by the air, or it may be sealed in a significant way. Our ignorance could destroy information. If you want to preserve it, circulate it, give it to the world, I think we need some friendly advice. Do you know anyone here whom we could trust to help?"

"Okay. You're right. I know a lot of people. I'll think of someone. For now, let's go out and celebrate your arrival with some Italian pasta and ice cream!"

CHAPTER FORTY-NINE

How Mandrake Found Out About Mary

It was by chance that Mandrake discovered Mary was his sister. During the process of selling Stonelea to the Mosaics, he had needed help from a solicitor. During a meeting at her office, Miss Evans had been called away momentarily, giving Mandrake's eyes time to stray over the papers on her side of the desk. A copy of Mary's birth certificate lay on the top. It showed her surname as Birch, the same as his. The date was correct too. When Miss Evans returned, Mandrake was agitated.

"Oh, oh, time for his next fix, I suppose," she thought. "I'd better get on with this or he'll behave oddly in here." She ignored his manner which had become even more distracted than usual. Tidying her desk at the same time, Miss Evans found the papers for Mandrake to sign. When she looked up, Mandrake was staring at her with an intensity that unnerved her.

"Yes?" she queried sharply, hoping to put him off. Mandrake leaned forward. His eyes filled with tears and he had difficulty speaking. He had a lump in his throat. He wanted to take her hand to ensure her attention, but experience had taught him not to touch. "Yes?" she asked again, her eyes shuttered, pushing him away with her voice.

Just for a moment, Mandrake had decided to trust this woman. Then the moment passed, pushed away by her harsh voice. He would have to find out for himself, yet in his heart, he felt he was already reunited.

Later on, he decided that he knew enough. Mary was his sister, but he wouldn't tell. She would not want him in her life, he'd only mess it up. Besides, in their brief dealings at High Table and more lately, with the house sale, she seemed to recoil from him. She didn't want him. She probably didn't even know that she had a brother or a sister for that matter; their sister Mandy. He had left for Vienna a few days later.

CHAPTER FIFTY

Mess In The Home, Mess In The Community, Mess In The World

After Clive and the police had left, Bruce tried to comfort his family. They did not yet know of the break-in at High Table. Jenny ran to him as Clive let her go. Pascal continued to cling to the table leg. Mary stood by the sink. She was full of shame and need. She had her back to the room and was gripping the edge of the draining board. Her knuckles were white and her eyes squeezed tight shut.

Bruce had never seen her like this before. He looked at the mess on the floor. Chunks of china lay strewn, splintered and powdered. He turned to Jenny.

"I'm going to sweep this up before anyone gets hurt." Jenny wanted to help and fetched the dustpan and brush. Bruce fetched newspaper and together they cleared the floor. At first, Mary and Pascal did not move. Then Mary left the room and went out into the garden. Pascal let go of the table and stood up to watch. When the broken china was wrapped in the paper and ready to be thrown away, he raised the lid on the peddle bin.

"Now," said Bruce, "what's been going on?".

"Mummy went mad," said Jenny. "She always does when she's trying to get Pascal to work."

"Does she usually go that mad?"

"Not that mad. She's never broken things before."

"What do you say, Pascal?" Pascal was looking down at his feet. He couldn't explain anything. "Why won't you do your work?"

"I can't," he said.

"Or won't," said Bruce. Pascal spun on his heel, turning his back on his father. Tears welled up in his eyes and he tried to swallow down the sobs that strained to come. "I think I'd better go and find Mummy. You two can watch telly." He turned it on. Two men were shouting at each other, about to fight. A woman, cowering in the corner and who had obviously been beaten, was screaming and begging them to stop. Bruce flicked to another channel. There was a news report about the discovery of a mass grave in Mexico. The reporter was describing the grief of those who thought it might contain the remains of their disappeared men. He flicked again. Soldiers swarmed up a bank, being fired on from a pill box above them. A further try brought into their home, a family who were quarrelling, at loggerheads, with no one listening to anyone else. He gave up, grabbed a dvd, set it running and went out into the garden.

Mary was vigorously weeding the vegetable patch.

"This chickweed comes up so fast," she said. Bruce went nearer to her.

"High Table has been broken into." Mary stopped weeding. "When Clive and I got there, Gemma was outside waiting for me. She had already called the police."

"Is there much damage? Was anything taken?"

"I don't know. The police arrived very soon after Clive and me. As they did, I suddenly had this great fear that you and the children were in danger. I think it was because I'd reported Mandrake's abduction last night that it put them on my side. I could hardly speak I was so worried. Clive helped and when they realised what I was on about, they didn't hesitate. But... what on earth were you doing?" Bruce felt anger rise in his belly as he asked this question, feeling worry for his restaurant and how he should be there.

"You just don't have a clue, do you?" said Mary. "You are out so much that you don't see it. Every time Pascal has anything to do regarding school, he becomes impossible. I can't even tell whether or not I'll be able to get him in the car to take him to school. I never have any problem getting him home though. You have been around when he won't do his reading, his writing and so on, but you don't seem to register how constant it is, or to mind for that matter.

"I've talked to Mr Croft, that's his headmaster in case you don't even know that..." and Mary too felt anger agitating her.

"Hold on Mary. Of course I know who Mr Croft is. You don't have to start on me!"

"Don't you dare say a word to wrong foot me! I'm telling you how difficult things are and the very fact that you don't know is part of the problem. You don't listen Bruce. You think you do but you don't. When I tell you about things - me, the children, something your mother said, it's not just for your amusement, or mine. I'm trying to get you to pay attention, to join in, to participate, to think through with me what needs to be done – for you to know about your family.

"You seem to hear but then you do absolutely nothing in response and neither does Mr Croft. He says that Pascal's perfectly all right at school and that I'm worrying without cause. No one, no one at all, has stopped for one minute longer than they choose, to help think this through. Pascal is utterly miserable. He begs me to keep him at home and I'd far rather do that than deliver him daily to a set-up that pays so little attention to what they're doing. But I can't. I have to go along with it and it's agony.

"Every time Pascal refuses to co-operate, I am filled with conflict. Yesterday began as a nightmare long before your drama with Mandrake and Clive, but there was never time to tell you. I just hoped it would go away. I'm always hoping it will go away. I don't think I can stand it any more, Bruce." Mary dropped her trowel back into the earth and shook down the weeds that she had gathered into a bucket.

"I'm sorry about the break-in, about Mandrake, about the awful time you had last night. I'm sorry and I'm worried. I feel that I should be supporting you through all this and I do. But I need support here too. I feel I'm always waiting for my turn. All the time, I know that Pascal has to go to school tomorrow and he's rarely completed his homework. I thought we placed importance on that too. I'm trying to give him boundaries, to show him that I won't give in however much he plays up, but it's wearing me out and underneath it all, I feel it's pointless."

"Is it so bad? Don't your friends have these battles with their children from time to time?"

"From time to time, yes, but not all the time. Not every day without change. Pascal is a different child during the holidays. He's happy, co-operative, relaxed, talkative, enthusiastic - all the things that come naturally to him. As soon as school is mentioned, he totally changes."

"Do you think he's being bullied?" Bruce wondered.

"I don't know what to think," said Mary. "How on earth am I supposed to know? He's only eight years old for heaven's sake. He's at a small village school where they claim to know and care for each child individually. How am I supposed to find out what the trouble is? I'm not there all day - the teachers are! Yet, they won't talk to me. I just get put off all the time and then I have to pick up the pieces."

"How long has it been this bad?"

"You know, part of me feels relieved that you're asking and part of me feels furious and frustrated that it's taken all this to get you to notice. I've been trying to tell you about it for such a very long time. Now you're listening, yet at the same time you've got to go back to High Table and sort things out there. I know you have to, but that leaves me alone again. Alone with this problem, alone with the children. Poor Jenny. It must be awful for her too. Do you realise that every weekend is the same? Everything is focussed on getting Pascal to complete his work. Anything else is secondary to that. What am I doing wrong? We used to be like this," Mary placed the palms of her hands together, "but now there is tension almost all the time. We are at war. Something's very wrong and I don't know what to do about it."

"Mary, stop! Why haven't we talked about this more? What's happened between us?" She shrugged, then clenched her fists and waved her arms in exasperation.

"Why look to me alone for an explanation of this? You should be answering this too!" She stepped off the vegetable bed onto the path and began to walk towards a stone bench set beneath the lilac bush. Bruce followed her. Nearby, the swing hung empty. They sat together. Mary sighed.

"I don't know. I keep waiting for a good moment, but there never is one. You don't ask either. It's very painful not being heard. I suppose that I don't put myself up for any more of it than I have to. You see, I absolutely know that something is wrong with Pascal, or the school or whatever. No one else does. I'm beginning to think that I may be going mad."

"Do you mean that?"

"It would be one way of explaining this. My view seems to be at odds with everyone else. Isn't that what insanity is? I am seeing a reality that is invisible to everyone else. Perhaps I am hallucinating. Perhaps it's Munchausen's Syndrome By Proxy as one dear friend hinted the other day when I tried to confide in him. Whoever I approach says the same range of things - that I'm intruding, that I'm expecting too much, that I'm not keeping boundaries, that I'm too rigid. You name it, I'm it - the cause. Anything but the possibility that I may be right and worth listening to. What do you think Bruce? Am I worth listening to?"

"I have always thought so," he said, touching her gently on her elbow. They fell silent. A blackbird began to sing.

CHAPTER FIFTY-ONE

Something Is a Whole Lot Better Than Nothing

After Clive left Stonelea with its broken china, he declined a lift back into town with the police. He wanted to walk. To begin with there was no pavement and he tucked himself into the greening hedgerow when an occasional car droned past him, disturbing dust. Clive was deeply preoccupied and did not notice the backdrop of sunshine and bird song.

He was thinking about Mary and her state of passionate anguish. He had not felt as passionate as that in his life, except for once, that time with Zorcia. Since he had led her into such folly and danger, he had felt nothing like it again. He had not cared about anything enough to want to throw down a dish, shout or cry. It looked painful for her and he wouldn't wish pain on anyone, but at the same time, it was so real. What was real for him? It made him feel half dead.

In all the years since Zorcia had been swept away in the helicopter, alternately waving and then wiping her eyes with the handkerchief that he had given to her at the last moment, he had never allowed himself to think of what might have happened to her. He couldn't bear it. The prospect was too painful. He skimmed across it in his mind knowing that to think of it would require him to face his own responsibility and desolation, let alone the possibility of hers.

His heart ached, reminding him of the empty space there. A part of him longed to feel wild with some emotion, but he didn't know how to go about it. Clive walked home to his flat, resigned to spending the afternoon alone.

CHAPTER FIFTY-TWO

The Currency of Truth

Pietze trusted De Vries and told Klara about him. He was a brilliant scholar and archaeologist who, like Pietze, had left mainstream academia. He was interested.

He arrived at the flat, smiling at Klara as he came up the stairs. She stood aside, beckoning him through the door, a tall, slight man in pale cottons and complicated sandals. Klara pulled the jar and little packages from the cupboard. Again, as she took them, she felt that same sense of well-being that had touched her before. She lingered before giving them to De Vries, enjoying the sensation. As he took them into his hands, he looked up at her. They were both experiencing the same thing. De Vries sighed deeply, joyfully.

"This is something very special," he said. He turned over the packages and took out the lens. "This does not surprise me but it delights me." He put it to his forehead, holding it above his nose, between his brows. He shut his eyes. If they had been open, he would have been looking straight at Klara. And yet, he could see her, changed in some way but not by age. She was kneeling back on her heels, hands resting upturned in her lap, serene. Light streamed from her as she steadily returned his gaze. He sensed that in some way he was seeing the future.

De Vries lowered the lens and opened his eyes. Klara was looking at him enquiringly.

"Did you see something?" she asked.

"Yes, but I can't say," he replied. "Let's see what the jar has to offer." After examining the seal minutely with a jeweller's eyeglass, he took notes. Then he pulled a penknife from his pocket and eased out a short, strong blade. Spreading a clean cloth onto the table and laying the jar on its side, he picked tiny chips out of the seal, working his way around the lid.

Klara and Pietze watched, their heads gradually moving closer to De Vries as he worked. "Hey! Give me some air, you guys!" They moved back, slightly startled to find how close they had drawn.

De Vries continued to pick. When he had worked his way around, he gathered up the cloth to contain the debris of his work and tucked it into his pocket.

"I'll want to look at everything," he said. Then he changed the blade to a long, flexible one and gently slid it down the side of the stopper until it was loose. He held the end up to Klara.

"Here you are." She grasped the lid. It came away sweetly. No genie coiled out in a puff of smoke or dust. The air was still. Inside the jar was a golden gleam. Klara turned the open end towards the men.

"Look," she said as they leaned forward.

"Oh this is just beautiful," said De Vries. He lifted up the jar, giving the open end a slight tap against the palm of his hand. Then he pulled on the contents. "This is gold sheet." His tone was of disbelief overturned. "And it's inscribed." He brought a small, intricately marked, golden script into the daylight. There were symbols, some kind of ancient writing Klara thought, and diagrams. "I do not know these symbols," De Vries said. "But look, in this one a person is writing. In this, people are talking. They are dressed differently from each other which may indicate communication between different communities or schools of thought." He examined further. "Here we are!" he exclaimed, excitement mounting in his voice. "This man here is looking at the sky. He is holding something to his eye. Perhaps it is a lens, or perhaps I just want it to be one. These images down here are similar to ones I have seen before in connection with the Dead Sea Scrolls which were discovered in caves around Qumran in the nineteen-fifties. As for these lenses, coming in the same consignment, put together by an unknown person or people, it is very interesting and excites my curiosity no end.

"I think this proves that the chase that Klara described was on account of the chest and not because of the girl. We must be very careful with these things. There are many forces active in this world. Some work for enlightenment, some to suppress. I know this because I have seen it first hand, not just heard or speculated about it.

"We are guardians of something that, until we know otherwise, we must protect from those who would stop at nothing to keep it hidden."

"Tell me about Qumran," asked Klara. The moment that De Vries had mentioned it, Klara had felt the same sense of peace and alertness that she experienced when touching the lenses and scroll.

"It was a community that existed before, during and for a short while, after Christ. It's in ruins now. The scrolls were found in fits and starts and went through many pairs of hands, in and out of museums and war zones. Some were destroyed before their value was appreciated. There's no definitive research or translations of the scrolls as far as I know. Some findings have been made public, but these seem to have been pieced together by deduction and assumptions born out of current, mainstream occidental thinking. This kind of thinking can discover much, but it has massive limitations too. A jig-saw that is made in such a way can turn out very different from the truth, especially if those who have commissioned its construction have previously dictated the contents of the picture."

"But why would anyone want to suppress the truth?" Klara asked.

"Not everyone has the strength to hear it," De Vries replied. "I'm talking about open mindedness versus rigid thinking. I'm talking about the way that information is used."

"Say more," said Klara. "Give me an example." She wanted to know and she liked to hear and see this man talking.

"Okay. Here goes. Suppose I believe something, let's say, that an apple is a good thing to eat. I'm healthy, I want others to be healthy, so I try to convince them to eat apples too. Then I start growing them to sell to people because it seems a good way to make my living. I tell more and more people of my beliefs in the value of apple eating and succeed in increasing my market.

"When I see that I'm loosing potential sales because of orchard pests, a flame of greed is awakened in addition to the practical business aspects. I want to be in complete control of my orchards. I set up a research project to solve the problem and come up with pesticides. I increase my yield and am now selling not only apples. I'm selling pesticides too. You can understand how things go on from here. By now, I have forgotten that my original aim was to improve people's health. The momentum is too great and I'm no longer in touch with my motives as I was once.

"Then questions form in the minds of some people. Do they need these many apples? Is the pesticide harmful to them? What will be the long term effects and so on. I don't like these questions. I like the way things are without them. I'm living well and I don't want that to change. Some people begin to reduce their apple intake or to buy organically grown ones. This has an impact on my turnover - apple turnover!" De Vries laughed, but Pietze and Klara did not understand the joke. They were Austrians, speaking in German and they were used to strudels. De Vries gave a little cough to help his joke to die. Then he continued.

"So, now my profits take a dive and I don't want this. I find ways to suppress, rubbish or confuse the information that jeopardises my plans."

"Are you saying that all this stuff contains information that could shed new light on the current, popular view of the past and that it would change our perspective and therefore affect our understanding of the present?" asked Klara.

"That's what it looks like to me," said De Vries. "It would explain the interest. People who have a benevolent interest in something don't behave in the ways you have seen. We have much to think about. For example, do either of you realise that possessing these things could be personally dangerous? Do you value the truth? Do you want to risk yourself in order to protect it?" He looked straight at Klara and then at Pietze. "I think that we need to talk this over right now."

Klara had no hesitation. "I want to do whatever it takes. This feels real to me. It's what I've been waiting for. It feels special. Here we are together. It could have been so different, yet this golden scroll and these lenses are with us for a reason. I brought them here and very quickly, I have found someone who knows how to proceed. This is better than hanging around my father's night club, treading a strange line between squalor and respectability. I'm taking part. This is my adventure."

"When I left Vienna," said Pietze, "I wanted to do something worthwhile, on my terms. I wanted to make my own life and to find a way to make it count. This may all come to nothing, don't forget, but for the moment, I too wish to join in."

"Then let us plan carefully," said De Vries. "We must work together to discover all we can, to protect these treasures and to find a way to share our discovery with who ever we feel we should."

"I'll tell you where I'm going to start," Klara said. "I've got nothing to offer here. When I've picked your brains, De Vries, I'm going to Qumran. That's my next move."

"Then let us make a plan," said Pietze. "A plan for the part that we each will play."

CHAPTER FIFTY-THREE

Walking With Intuition

For the whole journey to Qumran, Klara thought constantly and with longing of what it would be like. It felt good to be going there. She had resisted the conventional norms presented to her, but when asked why by her troubled parents, she had been unable to explain. Although she knew that she did not want to live like them, she could not say why or what it was that she did want. Now, as she travelled, she felt like an arrow passing clean through the air, heading for the bull's eye of her target - Qumran.

As she approached her destination, her driver offered her strange pretzels from a yellow and green packet with Arabic script. For mile after mile, the rough road snaked through dry land and she had a sense that she was coming home for the first time in her life. Looking up at the bare red hills on either side, Klara knew more clearly now than ever before that there was something here for her.

Occasionally, a car came towards them, hurtling along the road in a way that suggested little need of traffic awareness. Even with plenty of time to prepare for each other, the cars always seemed to wait until the last possible second before taking an emergency swerve. And from time to time by the road, a place to stop and eat, a road sign, a track turning into the desert, a woman walking, veiled, exotic, graceful. They whisked on past it all.

Near Qumran, Klara by-passed a hotel and found a place to stay on the outskirts of a Bedouin village. The house was tiny, a cube really, with rugs for comfort and a small cooking fire in the compound. A peaceful place, despite the sounds of talking and the playing of backgammon from her neighbours. And sitting there, in a place she had never much thought about, Klara anticipated that she would soon discover her purpose. She had left the precious artefacts with

Pietze and De Vries. They were intending to work discretely; Pietze to explore the story behind the lenses and De Vries to work on the translation. Klara wrote to them, telling them of her safe arrival.

After some weeks, nothing had happened. Klara had explored. She had breathed in the air of a new place, bathed in its sunlight, eaten its food, felt apart from the community and yet that she belonged in a way that other visitors did not. She began to wonder what she was doing. On an evening when logic prevailed, she stopped to think her life through and she had to admit to herself that, looked at by most people's standards, there was no way of explaining or validating her stay.

The next day, Klara tried an experiment. She left her lodgings and boarded a bus out of Qumran, taking all her luggage. She wanted to see how it felt. As the bus gathered speed out of the place, heading further and further away, her emotions began to churn. She could even feel the beginnings of panic. At a road side eating house, she got out. Immediately, her head began to clear and she became calm once more. She would have to go back.

There was a long wait for the return bus so Klara took a seat outside, feeling at peace again and smiled to herself as she sipped her tea and ate sweet cake.

She noticed a youth, a local by all appearance but not a person she had met in her village. He was watching her. When their eyes met, he smiled and nodded at her. Klara returned his gesture. He came over to her table, asking with his eyes for her final invitation to sit with her. Pulling out a chair for him, she nodded her assent.

Like so many Austrians, Klara spoke good English. Saluman was also able to speak a little. This sort of thing is a blessing for the English who can travel to some of the most remote places in the world and converse with others. Some argue that it makes them lazy, but perhaps it just leaves them free to think about other things such as inventing the Dyson vacuum cleaner. Whatever it means, what it also adds up to is that people whose first language is not English, but who can none the less speak it to some degree, can also travel to remote places and converse. So it was with Klara and Saluman.

When Saluman sat at her table, Klara felt recognition. What ever it was that she had come for, he had a part to play.

"I know you," he said.

"I know you," said Klara.

"Come with me," he said, getting up. He called to someone in the cafe and led Klara round the back where some camels were sitting. Salumen took Klara's pack and strapped it to one of the camels. He helped her on to another, showing her how to hook her leg around the front of the saddle. Then he mounted a third, leading the pack camel beside him. Klara noticed that water bottles and other bundles were already saddled up. She had never ridden a camel before although she could ride horses well. This was quite different. The range of lurching as the camel had stood up was extraordinary, but she had hung on and kept her balance. Now here she was, up high with a great view and a feeling of sheer delight. This was going to tax her body. It did not matter. Her heart was singing as she followed this young man out of the village and into the desert.

CHAPTER FIFTY-FOUR

Not So Tenacious After All

Tailing Mandrake had been a long shot. All the time she had kept tabs on him, Blanche had thought that it would probably lead to nothing. Now she had been proved right. The sous-chef had provided brief hope, with his mention of the key that Mandrake had shown him. But now that she had seen it for herself, that hope too had been shown to be false. Mandrake was just a loser and certainly altogether lost now, given the state he had been in a few hours ago.

Blanche had had his house searched when he had been living at Stonelea but there was nothing there, not even in the attic or the out buildings. She had spent enough time on this avenue. He was a friendless, homeless junkie and of no further consequence to her. If she was ever going to discover the whereabouts and contents of that chest, it would be by a different avenue. She informed Jovan that Mandrake and the trail were dead.

Blanche's indifference to death and to life lay like a dense, leaden blanket between her heart and mind. She had put it there in order to prevent her from feeling the hurt of her isolation. It was very effective. It kept her life on track and she was in control of it. She liked the security of its hardness beneath her thoughts.

Her thoughts informed her actions and together they got her what she wanted - power over people and objects.

CHAPTER FIFTY-FIVE

A Dream Realized In The Desert

Klara followed Saluman all afternoon. It was very hot. They stopped in a waddi to drink and rest. Saluman built a fire in the shade of a tall rock, cooking bread and vegetables. She lay in this shade too, easing her body into relaxation after the rigours of camel riding. She wondered where they were going but knew that she did not need to ask. Klara was being drawn across the desert like a pin to a magnet.

Later, with the sun much lower in the sky and the desert night about to swallow them up, they arrived at a tiny cluster of dwellings surrounded by vegetable plots and sparse, thorny trees. Goats browsed indifferently upon coarse weeds sprouting at the edges of outbuildings and gazed at Klara and Saluman as they stopped beside the well. Chickens scratched, running off, slightly flustered by their arrival. Saluman dismounted and handed the reins of his camels to a boy who had come out of one of the houses. Then he helped Klara off hers and the boy took them away. She was saddle sore, stiff around her hips and shoulders and elated. She stretched and rubbed the small of her back.

Saluman beckoned her into the smallest house, holding a piece of heavy cloth aside for her to enter. It consisted of one room, lit by slit windows high in the walls. The natural light was almost gone and a lamp had been lighted in anticipation of night. A fire-place took up one end of the room where the fire was alight and a woman made a gesture of welcome and returned to her tasks. Klara looked to the other end of the room.

As her eyes adjusted to the light, she could see a man sitting there. He looked biblical, serene and at peace. His eyes were lowered at first, but then he raised them and met Klara's eyes with his own, beaming a smile at her. She was enveloped in his loving welcome and total acceptance of her.

She went towards him. She held out her hands and he took them as she knelt down before him, filled with joy.

Klara knew that time was passing, but she could not assess its speed. She was engrossed in the experience of being embraced by light. She could feel herself expanding and being transformed. She had truly come home.

For the next five years, Klara lived there, spending her time in service to her teacher, a master at one with cosmic consciousness. She was given the opportunity to live life in ways that she could never have achieved without his guidance. Certainly no one had ever spoken to her before about the different planes of existence, of healing, of God consciousness or meditation without making it very clear that such things were akin to myth, illusion and superstition.

To Klara, a truth that withstood all her questions, doubts and explorations revealed itself moment to moment, enabling her to understand the heart of matters, where she recognised and experienced God's presence in herself and in everything else.

CHAPTER FIFTY-SIX

Bruce's Best Is Found Wanting

Bruce went back to his restaurant to sort out the break-in. He and Mary had agreed that the homework issue should be dropped for the day.

"How about going down to the stream for the rest of the morning? You and the children could build a dam. It's one of the first days of the year when it's warm enough to do it. I must get to High Table now."

"Okay," said Mary, "but don't leave me to sort this out alone. Promise me that you will help. I've come to the end of solo piloting."

"I promise," said Bruce as he left.

At High Table, the police had assessed the situation. Gemma was leading the clear up operation. Bruce felt so grateful to them all. Sergeant Palmer greeted him.

"We need to talk, sir. Somewhere quiet I think."

"Yes, we do," said Bruce. He took him to the store room by the kitchen. "Would this do?" As Palmer nodded, Bruce added, "I just need a few minutes to talk to my staff and see if we can catch up well enough to be in business by lunch time." He looked at his watch. "It's cutting it a bit fine, but if we change the menu and keep it simple, we won't have to cancel our bookings or turn people away. Anyway, they tend to respond favourably to a crisis. Thank goodness for the sun, we can sit them outside." He talked to his staff, thanking them and planning the day. Then he rejoined Palmer.

"This seems to be a straight forward break-in," he said. "We have had a series lately and this has the hallmarks of the same gang. We know who they are. Now we just need enough evidence that will stand up in court. It's frustrating to say the least. I see no connection with regard to the abduction you reported last night. However, I can tell you that I may have some news regarding that. I just have to wait for some further information before I can convey it to you.

"Now, there is also the matter of what happened at your house this morning, sir. As I am sure you will understand, it's a situation that didn't look too good and as a police officer, it's not something I can ignore or forget about. Your wife and children were very distressed. What was going on?"

Bruce told Palmer what happened after he and Clive had left that morning.

"I must confess," he added, "that I have been turning a blind eye. I've hardly had time to think about it. I haven't made time to think about it, but I'm beginning to realise that there has been a lot of tension around and I have been leaving it to Mary to deal with. I don't know how to help Pascal when he is so adamant, how to persuade him to co-operate. He's a bright little boy and he'll talk to anyone. He's full of ideas and he can read situations intelligently, but when he won't get on with his writing, I feel manipulated and that I'm not being strong for him, that I can't save him. I don't like it when I don't know what to do."

"I understand what you are saying only too well," said Palmer. "Has the word dyslexia ever been mentioned as a possible explanation for all of this?"

"He can't be dyslexic because he can read," said Bruce. "He doesn't like it, but he can do it."

"Dyslexia isn't just a matter of reading. It's a title for a whole range of learning difficulties, some of which are only very slight. But if those difficulties are ignored and the child not helped, all manner of troubles come. You describe Pascal's difficulties in a way that makes me wonder if this is what's causing the problem. And another thing - the way the school is handling it reminds me of my own family.

"My daughter Sophie is dyslexic. She had a terrible time when she began school. My wife and I experienced something similar to what you are describing. I'm not in a position to make a diagnosis. However, I do suggest that you investigate this possibility and investigate it very soon. Things aren't going to improve if you do nothing. If your son is dyslexic he needs help and support. He needs it whatever the cause of his unhappiness. He's crying for help. That puts you in the front line.

"If your school is half as intransigent as Sophie's was, you will meet with a lot of resistance, but you've got to sort this out. I don't want to start muttering things about 'at risk'. Still, after what I witnessed this morning, I would strongly advise you to talk things through with your wife and deal with this by facing it. Ask for help before you are made to take it."

Bruce was shaken. It had taken the view of an outsider to make him realise that what had been building up, was as a direct consequence of not facing the facts for himself. He had ignored them. It hadn't worked. They had not gone away, not by any measure.

"Yes. You are right," he said. "I'll ring up his headmaster when I get home after work."

"Think again," said Palmer. "What are your priorities? It seems to me that you have got a sufficiently dedicated and smooth-running team here. After work is not what I had in mind as a way for you to deal with this. Right now would be more appropriate. That's how urgently I view this matter. If you delay on this, then I cannot consider that your children are in a safe place. I don't want to take this any further, but I will unless you clearly indicate to me that you take this matter very seriously.

"According to 'the book', we should not be having this conversation. But we are. I'm taking a risk because there are some things that are more disruptive than the disruption itself, if you understand me. You can and must sort this out and I insist that you start today if I am to feel confident that I am helping you in the best way."

Bruce found this difficult to hear. He did not identify himself as a man who was not providing well for his children. Was it so easy to become a neglectful father and husband? He wanted to say something in his defence. He wanted Palmer to excuse him in the circumstances and to validate his good intentions and busy life. What had his priorities been? Couldn't Mary have done more? She looked after the children, he looked after the business. It was an arrangement that had fallen into place by unspoken agreement. He thought that she had been dealing with it.

"My wife...," he began, his desire to apportion blame betrayed in his tone of voice.

"I'm sure you've both done your best," said Palmer. Bruce struggled. It was hard to admit that his best was way short of what was needed. His shoulders drooped and he sighed, recognising the wisdom of the man before him.

"My poor little boy," he said. The words, catching in his throat which was tight with his conflict, came out squeaky and whispered.

"If it's any comfort," said Palmer, "it gets better from now on. However much people don't or won't understand, you can now be on your son's side, his ally. If dyslexia is at the bottom of all this, you will see that Pascal is right when he refuses his homework. He is right because it is true that he can't do it. Now he can have your support and your wife's support. You will be united, a team. No more divide and conquer, not from him or from the school. You will win through if you link up over this. Get a diagnosis. Find out what this is all about and don't wait for others to take the lead. You are his parents. You do it. Do it today."

"I'll go now." Bruce attended to his business and then went home.

CHAPTER FIFTY-SEVEN
There Are No Horizons

Fear of what others think, of being unable to live a worthy life, of being incapable of loving enough, of feeling pain; each interferes greatly with how we live our lives. These fears distance us from ourselves, are distracting, destructive and limiting. How do they come into being? How do we get them to go? Love your self. Know the roots of your motives.

Why have you chosen them? Do they serve you now as you thought they would? The road out of dark unhappy places is taken when the search for answers begins. Through peaks and valleys it can lead from sorrow to enlightenment. The word guru means 'dispeller of darkness' and such a person can light the way, offering a fast track out of the bondage of ignorance, a way to freedom. This is the help that Klara was willing to receive.

When she became self realized, Klara lived according to a reality that was completely new for her. She knew her own glory and worth and that of all else. She was engaged with a super-consciousness that existed within her and beyond her. She understood what it meant to be at one with all creation, both seen and unseen. She knew herself without limits and could thus create her life with intention. She called upon the source of all love, allowing it to flow through her and to find expression in all that she thought, said and did.

When it was time to leave her guru and to return to Milan and Vienna, Klara made her choices as she had always done, by intuition. As a child, she had been called impulsive or selfish when she had insisted on doing certain things in certain ways. Now, this way was tempered with understanding. During her time with her guru she had learned to trust the process completely.

In her absence, Pietze and De Vries had worked hard on the scroll and the lenses. And in all that time, they had been unable to find any information as to how the lenses could have been constructed. They had tried to match the little history that they had and the events that had led to them coming into their possession, with what they could discover about the likely timings of lens-making technology. It seemed that these lenses had been made long before any others previously known to be connected with Middle Eastern scientific instruments.

The scroll gave instructions on the use of the lenses and many diagrams of constellations. It described how different combinations of lenses would reveal different views of the heavens, both literally and metaphorically. The mood and level of perception of the user, would also affect what could be seen.

Both men had experienced this for themselves, discovering how at first, the excitement of their work had given them tunnel vision when looking through the lenses. As they had gained understanding of the instructions and confidence in their extraordinary contents, their vision had expanded, giving them a multi-dimensional view of everything they had chosen to examine. Despite this, how they had been made was still a mystery.

Like true scholars, Pietze and De Vries had documented their work and were intending to publish it anonymously on the internet. They wanted to share this discovery with the world. They were waiting for Klara.

"If we are careless with this information," said Pietze, "it will be taken into obscurity again."

"If we keep it, it will be in obscurity," said De Vries.

"If we keep it for just a little longer, the time will be right to release it," said Klara. "Then it will bring the greatest benefit of all." The two men looked at Klara. She was radiant.

"Okay," said Pietze, "let's say we keep it for now. I have to say, Klara, that there is something about you that is beyond argument. What have you discovered?"

"Yes," said De Vries, "I agree that we hang on to this for now, with a view to bringing it out later. Like Pietze, I can see that you have also been having an extraordinary time, Klara. What have you been doing? Whatever it is, it suits you. Can I have some too?" He remembered what he had seen the very first time that he had looked into one of the lenses.

CHAPTER FIFTY-EIGHT

Natural Synchronization

Before leaving Qumran, Klara had written to Elsa who was now a teacher in a secondary school.

> My Dearest Elsa,
>
> I expect to come back to Vienna very soon. You may tell this to anyone you feel needs to know.
>
> There is something that I ask you to do. It needs to be done at the right time. You are the person that I trust to do it.
>
> Following this letter, a parcel will arrive. Please put the contents into that old chest that you have stored with you. The lock will close for you. Then take it to the following address,
>
> Stonelea, Victoria Road, Salterton, Near Salisbury, Wiltshire, England. Please do this on November 8th, very early in the morning. At that time, the house will be empty and unlocked. Take it to the top of the house and leave it there. All will be well. All is well!
>
> I won't explain anything to you in a letter. I know that we will have time to talk soon and then we can talk for as long as we like. I have discovered much in my absence and look forward to sharing it with you when we meet on our joint return to Vienna.
>
> I love you,
>
> from your sister,
> Klara.

This letter for Elsa arrived just as she was making her final plans to take a party of school children to England for a tour of cathedrals. Their visit to Salisbury was set for 7th November. They were to stay the night in a converted manor house near Heale. When she looked at her map, it was almost next door to Salterton. Klara was right. This would be possible and she would do it for her.

Elsa went straight out across the park to Wien Nachts to talk to Klara's parents.

CHAPTER FIFTY-NINE

Croft Is Disturbed

The telephone rang just as his wife had dished up the pudding. It was an egg custard.

"Who on earth can that be at this time on a Sunday?" queried Mrs Croft as she helped herself to a little extra skin.

"Who indeed?" Mr Croft retorted, complacently pouring some cream into his bowl. Mrs Croft went to answer.

"It's for you," she said, returning to the dining room. "A Mr Mosaic. I tried to put him off, but he's determined," she added conspiratorially.

"What on earth can he want? I spoke to his wife only yesterday evening and we sorted everything out. Everything."

CHAPTER SIXTY

Bruce And Mr Croft Go A Few Rounds

When Bruce arrived home, the house was empty. The kitchen table had the remains of picnic makings all over it. At least the cheese and salami had been put back in the fridge, leaving only rind and wrappings.

"No health and safety gold star for this kitchen," he muttered as he tidied. He made a cup of coffee and sat with it in the garden, enjoying the chance to sit quietly in the middle of a Sunday, even on such a one as this. Usually he was working frantically at this time. He thought further about his conversation with Palmer. He thought about Pascal's school. He hardly knew the place. Mary dealt with all that, leaving him free to develop the business on behalf of his family. Why was this up to him too? In these times of equality, why was the ball now in his court?

Bruce tried to remember how things had happened. It was true what Mary had said this morning. They hardly ever did talk, not at depth. Was it also true that he didn't listen? What difference did it make anyway? He wasn't the only one who made decisions around here. Mary made masses of them without reference to him. Take the new washing machine, for example. She had just chosen one and gone out and bought it and now, there it was, in the utility room, working as always. And he made decisions every day that did not directly concern Mary. His menu he discussed with his chef. His cash flow he discussed with his accountant. His staff he discussed with... he discussed them with Mary.

Last November, just after they had moved into Stonelea, there had been that crisis with Gemma. He had needed to talk it through no end of times. In spite of all there was to do in their home, Mary had always been there for him. She had even made those phone calls to the Citizens Advice Bureau and then spent hours negotiating legal aid for the court case.

She had had to be very tough at times. It had helped Gemma to keep at work and he had kept a valuable employee. Mary had understood this and devoted a lot of time to helping the situation.

He could see that he had been unapproachable over anything other than High Table matters. It seemed that there was now a backlog for him to deal with and he would begin with a telephone call to Mr Croft.

He went into the house. First he phoned Gemma to check that they were managing. They were and he reiterated his thanks, expressing his hope to join them later. Then he phoned Mr Croft whose manner was brusque, although he tried to hide it with a friendly approach.

"Good afternoon Mr Mosaic," he said. He had taken a quick bite of his egg custard and he spoke through his clearing mouth.

"Good afternoon," answered Bruce. Having got this far, he realised that he had not ordered his thoughts and could not decide how to proceed. There was a short silence. Then Mr Croft spoke again,

"This is an unusual time for a parent to call me. I do hope that there is nothing wrong, Mr Mosaic."

"Oh no. Nothing too bad." It is bad. It is bad, he thought to himself, trying to find a better way to continue. "It's Pascal. Mary and I have had a talk. He is not getting on at school as we would expect. Time is moving on and we think that he should be settled at school by now."

"I quite agree with you, Mr Mosaic. In fact it is time that he realised that there is a certain amount that we all have to do each day and that he is no exception. As I told Mrs Mosaic yesterday," this was spoken pointedly, "I am intending to speak to Mrs Windspill tomorrow." Bruce wondered who this Mrs Windspill could be. "We will try to find a way to get this message across to him. We have this sort of thing from time to time with our children at school. We usually find a way to persuade them to join in. Tell me, does Pascal like computers?"

"Yes."

"Well, what often works with children who seem to think that they can take their time with their work, is to tell them that they can't play on the computers until they have completed it. I think that the time has come to talk to Pascal in this way and see if we can't jolly him along with a bit of a carrot and a bit of a stick."

"Pascal doesn't like that sort of approach," said Bruce. I know that much he thought, recalling many failed attempts at bribery that he had made in the past.

"Well, this is where I think mistakes have been made," Mr Croft broke in. "You and Mrs Mosaic may choose to keep off problem areas at home, but Pascal must face the, shall we say, the less exotic aspects of life at some point." Mr Croft's tone had become offensive. He was trying, almost successfully, to take control of the situation and to cut off what Bruce had to say. Bruce could feel himself wavering – perhaps he wasn't bringing his son up the right way.

"Do you think it could be dyslexia?" Bruce blurted out. There was a pause of several seconds. When Mr Croft spoke again, his tone was offended and icy.

"Mr Mosaic, dyslexia is a very rare condition. In all my years as a teacher and, for my sins that is quite a few, I have not come across more than two or three children with it. I assure you that Pascal is not one of them. He simply needs to knuckle down and to be shown that this is expected of him by everyone who is responsible for his care."

"I believe that my wife has spoken to you of our difficulties at the weekend and in the evenings concerning homework. You seem to be implying that this is a parent/child discipline problem, but I assure you," Bruce paused after the use of these words in order to give them emphasis, "I assure you that we have no difficulties in gaining Pascal's co-operation at other times. I was talking to the parent of a dyslexic child today and he suggested that we should explore this possibility further. That is why I am speaking to you. It is an urgent matter."

"With respect, Mr Mosaic, there are a lot of parents at the moment who believe that their children are dyslexic at the first sign that they cannot keep up with their class. It makes a simple explanation for having an under-achieving, wilful or lazy child. Parents of dyslexic children are not in a position to behave like part-time educational psychologists."

"Well in that case, I would appreciate it if we could put the ball in motion for Pascal to see an educational psychologist who is qualified to give a diagnosis. Talking to his teacher is important, but I believe that this has gone far enough now and that much more needs to be done. I am sorry for interrupting your day off. I have to confess that life has been a bit hay-wire for the last twenty-four hours and I had rather lost track of time."

"Ah, there you are!" Croft responded, quick as a striking snake. "That's what the trouble is. Children are very sensitive to disruption and Pascal is responding to that. Let's wait a little longer and see how he is when his home-life settles down again."

"You are right, Mr Croft. Children are very sensitive. I do not seem to have made things clear to you. Part of the disruption that I'm talking about is the effect of Pascal's long term distress on the whole family. If you are unwilling to offer more support than this, then I see no reason to continue sending my children to your school. The education authority can ask for my reasons and I will be sure to give them plenty."

There was silence down the line. Bruce felt his stomach knotted with anger at this man's intransigence. No wonder things had got so bad. Croft was simply stunned and could think of no further way of fending off this overwrought father.

"Well, Mr Mosaic. Thank you for sharing your concerns with me. I will consider what you have said and decide whether any further action needs to be taken."

"When you inform me of what that action will be, I will send my children back to your school. For now, I believe that my family needs a complete rest from all this and I will ensure that they take one until we all know what plans can be made. Thank you for your time, Mr Croft. Good bye." Bruce put down the receiver and began to gather himself together to return to work.

CHAPTER SIXTY-ONE

Denial Denied

L ater, when Bruce came home, Mary and the children had enjoyed their day. The dogs lay on the grass in the last of the afternoon sun, dozing and restful after hours of adventure and paddling in the stream. The children were playing, Pascal with lego and Jenny was drawing whilst Mary made supper. The atmosphere was calm and happy. At this angle, just in the corner under the fridge, Bruce could see a chip of white china. Otherwise, there was nothing in this scene to even hint at what had befallen this room earlier in the day.

After they had greeted one another, Bruce took Mary aside and told her about his talk with Mr Croft. Mary was both pleased and scared by what she heard. The prospect of such a rest was blissful, like the prospect of the school holidays. They could all go in to High Table and help Bruce if he wanted them to. She did not like the thought of being the next one to speak to Croft. She anticipated that she would hedge if the phone rang. Still, at least for twenty-four hours, she could count on being in harmony with her children, just as they had been today, once the school bogey-man had been removed.

CHAPTER SIXTY-TWO

How Mary Finds Out About Mandrake

On Monday morning, Bruce set off for the restaurant. Mary and the children luxuriated in an extra morning in bed. They brought her books and they lay together, cuddling, reading and dipping bananas into cereal packets, eating happily.

Sergeant Palmer came round to High Table. He and Bruce went over some details regarding the break-in. Then Bruce told him about his conversation with Croft.

"Have you anything to tell me about our abductee?" Bruce asked. Before Palmer could reply, Mary and the children arrived. Mary was shy of Palmer, considering how things had been when they had last met, but he greeted her warmly and she began to relax again.

"Sergeant Palmer was about to tell me about Mandrake," said Bruce. "Have you got news?" he asked, turning to Palmer.

"Yes. He was admitted to a hospital in Eastbourne in the early hours of yesterday morning. His name and lack of personal identification has caused some delay. As you would agree, Mandrake is an unusual name. It's not his real name. His real name is Robin Birch."

"How extraordinary!" exclaimed Mary. "Birch is my name too."

"Your maiden name?" asked Palmer.

"No, that was Hiscox. Birch is the name on my birth certificate. I'm adopted you see." Palmer nodded.

"There's a coincidence," said Bruce. The inflection in his tone implied an end to the discussion. Mary's lips tightened.

"No, this is no coincidence. This is something more than that. I feel it."

"Perhaps," said Bruce guardedly, "but to be fair, you have always had this thing about your relations and hoping to come across them. It's a natural thought, but so unlikely to be true."

"Why so?" Mary demanded of him. Emotions began to intrude. How could he threaten to humiliate her like this, and in front of Palmer too? She just wanted to have this possibility heard.

"Well, it's just not logical, is it? Here you are, living in the same area, buying his house, serving him in the restaurant. It's just too obvious."

"Stranger things have happened," said Palmer. Tears of relief sprang to Mary's eyes. "You can always look into it if you want. He's very ill apparently, although he turned the corner between life and death last night. You could go and see him. You would know better than I if he has friends, but remember that on Saturday night, when he was in such trouble, it was you that he turned to. This is a mighty big world, yet people do find each other in it and then they can be heard exclaiming on the smallness of it."

Bruce looked at Mary. He recognised the glow in her eyes. It came when she was absolutely determined to do something. If she intended to follow this through, he would be unable to hinder her. He wondered where befriending a drug addict would lead. A feeling of dread edged in. Then he remembered what Mandrake had said, about him having something of his. Despite his resistance, he felt excited.

"I've just thought of something. Mary, do you remember how mystified and worried we were on Saturday night, trying to make sense of what Mandrake could have been referring to, you know, about me having something of his?"

"Do you suppose he knows?" she asked eagerly. "Could he know? Why didn't he approach me?"

"Perhaps he has as far as he felt able. Would you approach anyone as a long lost relative if you were in his state?" asked Palmer.

"I saw the name Birch on the sales papers for the house," said Bruce, "but I didn't think anything of it."

"Bruce, I've got to go and see him," Mary stated. "The children will be okay with you for the day, won't they? If I don't follow this through, something very special to me may be missed!" Turning to Palmer she asked, "Is there any difficulty with you over this?".

"This whole situation is irregular, but then show me one that isn't. If we're looking to get people's lives straight, then going to him could be very important for you both – but do consider how ill he is. You know enough about him to understand that he will now be in withdrawal. However, what better time to have a person by your side to help. Remember though, he may not be your brother. If you go to see him and he feels supported by you, then for his sake, you need to have thought through what you will do if you are unrelated."

"We are. I just know it," said Mary.

"I know you do. On that basis, go ahead, take care and watch yourself, because the strength of your conviction is so great right now, it is even more important that you protect yourself and Mandrake from the consequences of the unexpected."

"Yes. Okay," she said, intending to do her best to think it through. This would be difficult for her because she had no basis from which to be 'sensible' about it.

CHAPTER SIXTY-THREE

No Collusion For Croft

At school that morning, Mr Croft noticed the absence of both Mosaic children. At break time, he wandered across the playground to Mrs Windspill who was supervising the children. Most of them were playing together, involved in physical activity of some sort or another, letting off steam.

Mrs Windspill was holding the hand of a girl of about six, who stood close to her teacher, sucking her thumb. As Croft approached, she hugged up even more.

"Ah, Dorothy. I expect you've noticed that we're missing Pascal and Jenny Mosaic," he began. Mrs Windspill nodded. "I'm afraid there's been a bit of a silly misunderstanding with the parents. They are insisting that Pascal is given some special attention and have withdrawn both children until this is arranged." Dorothy Windspill had a lot to say about Pascal. She had made several attempts to gain Norman Croft's attention, without success. Now perhaps his attention had been seized from a different quarter. She knew Norman well enough not to waste an opportunity to talk to him, even if it was a rather poor one. He had probably approached her whilst she was on playground duty with the precise intention of keeping their talk brief and shallow. Still, this was a start.

"Did they describe the type of special attention that they believe he needs?" she asked.

"Something on the lines of an educational psychologist, if you please!" he exclaimed, prompting Dorothy to share his ridicule and outrage. Dorothy did not.

"I think that could be appropriate. You may recall that I have had concerns about his progress and attitude for some time now. I have expressed these to you. We have been here, or something like it before, Norman. Think of Ben Thomson." Croft winced. "And what about Sophie Palmer? Those are two children who have both gone on from this school under a cloud, only to be given exactly this sort or special attention at their next schools and both with quite clear results that they were special needs. It doesn't exactly do us credit, does it?"

"Credit is the relevant word here, Dorothy. Our budget is stretched to breaking point. How on earth are we to find resources for special needs provision on top of everything else? Besides, it all comes out in the wash. We have a formula of tradition, routine and clear boundaries here. I see no need to change that and begin a whole lot of precious coaching for those who could fit in if they tried." Dorothy looked at her watch and then blew the whistle.

"Time's up!" she called to the children and she looked piercingly at Croft.

CHAPTER SIXTY-FOUR

Taking A New Road

Mary set off for Eastbourne. Bruce had made her a feast. As she drove, she ate and enjoyed the radio - her choice uninterrupted. She relished every glorious mile.

Cow parsley frothed in the hedges. The little dishes of elderflower blossoms were just beginning to show. Mary delighted in the way they grew, horizontal and yet uplifted.

She could not remember when she had last had a day like this. A day for her to follow through something entirely on her own behalf. Of course, being married to Bruce, having a home and children were also on her behalf, but they all required a kind of focus that was away from her. Her delight was in giving to them and receiving from them and that was as much as she deserved to desire. But there was this side of things too, the side that was not centred on family and home. The side that concerned her alone, whoever she might be.

Ever since she had married, she had put all her attention on home and family. Bruce had had his work. Her work, her wish, had been to provide the best she could in terms of love, attention and comfort. She had wanted to welcome her children into the world and show them how to live in it. She had tried to ensure that they lacked for nothing that was within her power to provide. So far, it had been very, very demanding. She had become absorbed in it, enveloped in it, identified with it. Today, she might meet her brother. Would such a meeting make her a different person?

"A brother, a brother and me, a sister!" she hoped. She hoped very much.

CHAPTER SIXTY-FIVE

Enough Pain

After the extraordinary events of the weekend, Clive was glad to go back to work for an early shift on Monday morning. He had arrived home very tired after his walk. His flat, empty for almost twenty-four hours, seemed to hold nothing for him, not even a vague sort of welcome on his return. He had walked around it, feeling lost.

"Bleak, oh so bleak," he had found himself saying for most of the afternoon. By evening, he was feeling truly depressed and had no energy with which to attempt an improvement. A companion, even one he didn't like much, would at least have been more stimulating than this – a distraction. He thought about the Mosaics. He had stood by them last night, even rescued Bruce and for all that, here he was, alone again.

He was more self sufficient than many men, although he had always wanted to marry, make a home and have children. He was good with them. He liked them and they liked him. He wasn't scared of them. But he had never trusted himself again after what happened between him and Zorcia. Before leaving for work he looked about his flat. It was functional. It was useful. It was there. He quite liked it, but he didn't love it. What did he love? He felt as if his life had been put on hold.

"How did it happen? Oh, so bleak, so very, very bleak," he groaned.

CHAPTER SIXTY-SIX

No More Nightmare

Zorcia went to the mountains for the day. She found her usual spot. It was isolated and full of peace. The ground was damp from the shade and the recently melted snow, so she sat on some low rocks, leaning back against a tree. This was her first outing of the year. For the first time since the autumn, she could feel the warmth of the sun on her face and hands when it dappled through the opening leaves on the birches above her.

She sat quietly, trying not to reflect on the awfulness of the winter that had just passed. The trees rustled. The breeze was quite strong, but here, sheltered by the rocks, she felt warm and safe. It was so good to be alone for once. She drank from her bottle and fell into a doze and a vivid dream.

She was standing by a river. On the opposite bank, a young woman was calling her name and beckoning. Zorcia felt a great desire to go to her yet did not want to get into the water. She felt frightened that if she did not go, she would lose. She began to panic, breaking into a run along the river bank.

The woman waited, nodding and continuing to beckon. Round the bend of the river, there was a beautifully arched, stone bridge. There was someone walking across it to meet her. It was a man. It was her lover.

Zorcia awoke suddenly. She felt at peace and as if something wonderful was going to happen. She took her bottle and tipped the contents out before returning it to her pocket. The sight of that clear liquid soaking in to the ground, beyond her reach, thrilled and frightened her. Perhaps this time she would get through. She drew a deep breath, lifting her gaze from where it had become fixed in the heart of a shiny yellow flower and looked up to the sky.

195

CHAPTER SIXTY-SEVEN

Coming Home In A Strange Place

As Mary entered the hospital, anxiety came upon her. There was so much at stake. Would they let her in if she wasn't a relation? Would she have to bluff and lie? In her head, she held an outraged exchange with a bossy nurse who would not let her pass. She felt angry that she might be stopped. Didn't they realise what this meant?

Then, without hindrance, she found herself approaching Mandrake's bed. For the first time in all the years in which their paths had crossed, Mary took the time to look carefully at this person lying before her.

"My brother, my brother," she whispered.

His breathing was noisy and laboured. He had a drip going into his left foot. The sheet, white and stiff, was folded neatly across him. He was probably wearing no clothes. Down his arms, which rested on the sheet, were the scars and injuries of addiction - sites of tired, infected and damaged veins. His shoulders were bruised and his face swollen, with stitches above his left eye. His hair was matted. Was he asleep? Was he unconscious?

Mary took a chair and sat beside Mandrake. She had her back to Bob Hodges. He was sitting beside his bed, watching. Mary took Mandrake's calloused hand in hers. She felt such a link with this man that it fed her certainty further. Could she feel all this if it wasn't true?

Mandrake stirred a little and then became quiet. A faint smile touched his face.

"She's here," he heard Gwendolyne saying. "She's here and you'll never have to be apart again."

Mary sat with Mandrake for hours. She thought of nothing other than the fact of their reunion. Sometime when he was better, they would talk about everything. For now, all she had to do was to be there for him. She went to telephone Bruce. She told him that Mandrake was indeed her brother, that he was very ill and that she was going to stay with him.

Bruce felt outraged. This did seem an awful lot for him to carry on top of what had already happened, but his protestations made no useful impression on his wife. She had never let him down like this before and he hoped she would not make a habit of it. He had backed her to the hilt over the school business and now he had all that to deal with plus the break-in, his business, the house, the dogs, just for starters. Mary was unmoved.

"Bruce, this is a one-off. If I come home just to relieve you all of having to think about the things that I usually deal with, I honestly believe that Mandrake could die. He's my brother, Bruce. He needs help and I can give it to him."

"Then what?" Bruce demanded. "Will you be telling me he's got to live with us next?"

"Who knows? Let's just take it one step at a time. I'm doing what I know to be right. Thank God you called the police, Bruce - that was right too. I really cannot think of anything you can say to me now that could convince me to come home to all of you. This will just make me a little later than first planned. It will cause you just a fraction, if any, of the harm that it could cause to Mandrake if I were to leave him now. I love you all, that's the point." She put down the phone and returned to Mandrake.

Bruce held the dead receiver in his hand, taking in its unchanging shape and the cool, dark grey plastic, unmoved by the content of the conversations it delivered. He replaced it, feeling cross.

CHAPTER SIXTY-EIGHT

Invisible Mending

On Klara's return to Vienna, her mother greeted her whole-heartedly. Her father however, was hurt by the minimal communication during her five year absence and by her failure to have used her time constructively. It was true that she looked good, although in his eyes, she had always been beautiful. Now she was living with them again. How was she going to survive in the future if she just sat about and glowed all the time? Klara offered him reassurance, yet he could not accept it. No one he knew had ever managed by taking life as it comes, having faith and so forth. Forward planning and conformity were required, then everyone knew where they were. He was worried for her.

Shortly after her return when the initial fuss had died down, she had told him that she had some work to do and asked if she could do it in her old room. Of course he had agreed, but when it came down to it, she was not making something, or studying, or corresponding. She was doing nothing that remotely resembled a decent days work. She was meditating and contemplating she said. 'Attuning herself to the life-force.' 'Communicating with other people telepathically.' And what was to become of that? How would she know when to stop? Would the telephone ring? How would he know when it was all over to her satisfaction?

She was still on friendly terms with Elsa. The two young women saw a lot of each other, as they always used to do. Come to think of it, his wife had been joining them. All three of them seemed mighty pleased with themselves. Here he was, working as hard as ever. Who was pleased with him?

CHAPTER SIXTY-NINE

Mutually Beneficial

Bruce called Clive and told him of what had happened since the row in his kitchen. The contrast between the sudden enrichment to the Mosaics life, for all the confusion it was bringing, to the emptiness of his own seemed all the greater. He longed to belong to someone in this way. He longed more than ever before.

"Do you want me to come and stay while Mary is away?" he asked. "I've got an afternoon shift tomorrow, then two days off. I could keep the kids company while you're at work." Bruce leapt at the offer.

"Clive, you are being the dearest friend. If I had another adult to share this with, it would make a huge difference."

"You're on," said Clive and began to pack his bags.

CHAPTER SEVENTY

Finding Out

Bob Hodges tried to engage Mary in conversation. He had been watching her, on and off, since her arrival earlier in the day. His daughter and grandson had paid a brief visit but with him being only four, it had been impossible to chat for long. He was glad they'd come though. He knew for himself from the time when his wife had been so ill, how lonely it could be sitting beside a sick-bed and even more so by a death-bed.

"Have you come far then?" he asked Mary's back view. She turned her head a little in acknowledgement.

"From Wiltshire," she said, turning away again. She wanted simply to be with Mandrake, to think just of him, to be there. She had no wish to discuss her journey, which route she had taken or how the weather had been. She was sure that this was where the conversation would lead if she joined it.

"I feel very close to him, you know," said Bob. That surprised Mary and she turned to face him without further thought. Her face made a question. "Last night, we both hit the pits. There was a nurse here who helped us through. She's special. If she's on tonight, I'll show you. You are staying, aren't you?"

"Yes. I am. He's my brother." Saying these words to a stranger made them all the more real. "He's my brother," she repeated and turned back to Mandrake.

That evening, the nurse who had so helped Bob and Mandrake the night before, was on duty again. She wore the badge and belt of a trained nurse, but she was obviously not in charge of the ward. She worked quietly at their end. She did not shout out or at any one, refer to individuals as 'we', issue strident instructions or turn a deaf ear as Mary had experienced when having her babies. Even without Bob pointing her out, Mary thought that she would have noticed her.

In the early hours of Tuesday morning, Mary awoke with a jerk as she fell forward onto Mandrake's bed. She looked at him. Little beads of sweat had appeared on his face. His colour was pallid and he was breathing differently. He became a little restless and began to mutter and move. Within moments, he was distressed, moving his whole body in the bed. Mary was frightened that he would dislodge his drip or knock himself on the railings on the sides of the bed. She went to look for a nurse. A quick scan of the ward was all she could allow herself before returning to Mandrake.

Mandrake's distress increased and Bob woke up and pressed the bell for him. At this time of night it made no sound, but lit up a red light above their section of the ward. A red light for stop. A red light for danger. Why didn't someone come? Mary didn't know what to do.

"Try holding his feet," suggested Bob. "That's what the nurse did last night and it seemed to help him through." Mandrake began to make horrible noises of suffering with his voice. Mary hesitated, full of doubt. "Try. It can't make it worse, surely."

Mary walked to the end of Mandrake's bed and held his feet. She felt silly and worried. She held her palms gingerly against his soles and hoped like mad that something would happen soon to calm her brother. The feeling of her closeness to Mandrake increased. It bubbled up through her body, running down her arms and through her hands. It felt good. She felt heat emanating from her. Mandrake stilled.

Mary became aware of a person standing beside her. It was the nurse that Bob had pointed out. She was looking at Mandrake and looking at her. She was smiling gently. Mary began to let go of Mandrake's feet.

"Stay with him, it's helping," the nurse said. "He needs medication too just now, but if you can support him in this way it will make all the difference. Please could you stay with him while I fetch his next injection?"

Mary agreed, continuing to hold on to Mandrake. She felt rather cut off from him now. He stirred and she was anxious that he would become agitated again. The nurse returned with an assistant and after making some checks and telling Mandrake what she was doing, she injected something into the drip.

"You're doing fine," she said to Mary.

"But how?" she asked. "How could holding his feet make all that difference?"

"There are many ways for us to help one another and some of them come so naturally that we hardly think about it."

"Holding someone's feet isn't natural, is it?" Mary asked, baffled.

"What were you feeling while you were doing it?" the nurse asked. Mary considered. She recalled the sensation of closeness and peace that she had experienced. She smiled inwardly.

"I felt good," she answered. "I felt that I was doing something odd, but that it was right."

"You were giving him healing," said the nurse. "You've got the gift of healing."

"What do you mean?"

"You held this man's feet with compassion. That's all it takes to make a start." Mandrake lay resting again. He was desperately pale, his eye-lids so dark in their sockets and with shadows of green about his nostrils, lips and forehead, although he was no longer sweating or distressed in his breathing.

"Could we talk about this more?" Mary asked. "I'm curious."

"I'd like that," said the nurse, "but right now, I have to work my shift. Your brother is comfortable for the moment. This would be a good time for you to have a break. The hospital canteen is open all through the night. I can give you an access ticket. How about some food and then a sleep in the relative's room? You can pull the chairs out into beds. There's only one other person staying tonight, so there's plenty of space.

"In the morning when I've finished, we can talk. I'll call you if there is any change." Mary looked at Mandrake. She felt very tired and hungry. She had had nothing to eat or drink since she arrived. She agreed to take a rest and so prepared to leave.

"By the way," said the nurse as she wrote out a chit, "my name is Julia."

After a light and dream-filled sleep, Mary awoke as Julia touched her firmly on her shoulder. She had brought two cups of tea. There was no one else in the room and morning had come. Mary sat up with a start, trying to force herself awake, pulling the blanket from her and preparing to get up. Her thoughts were all of Mandrake.

"Is he all right?"

"Yes, he's doing well. There's no need for you to get up. I've finished my shift and have come to talk with you as we agreed. What do you want to know?"

"I don't know really. I don't know which questions to ask. I'm still sleepy. Let's see. Well, how did you know that I was healing Mandrake?"

"Because I'm a healer and I recognised the effect that you were having by holding his feet in that way."

"How does it work?"

"Do you remember what I said last night about compassion?" Julia asked. Mary nodded. "Well, I can tell you what the teaching and experiences I've had, and what the observations I've made, have taught me. I have learned that love is the essence of our existence. I don't mean the soppy sort, you know, the sort that makes us into doormats and fakes. I mean the strong sort. And when we reach out with that kind of love, we affirm the interconnectedness of all things. When we pull away from each other by, let's say, judging or competing, we are acting out of fear and we make ourselves separate from each other. Buying into separation takes us against our basic design. If you or anyone for that matter, goes against a design, that stresses it and causes unnatural wear, breakage, dysfunction. There are examples of this all around us.

"Healing points us back to unity. Healing energy communicates, without the need for words, with all living things, even rocks, at a deep level." Mary felt that deep level stirring within her. She felt hungry for more information.

"How do you do it?"

"It's a simple matter of making a link between the source and the patient. The healer is the link, like a set of jump leads for a car when the battery has gone flat. I have been taught to make that link in safety, both for myself and for those I help. I could put you in touch with a teacher."

"I'm interested, but this is all very new. I need to think. I'm exhausted. I've just had some of the strangest few days of my life."

"If you would like, I could give you some healing now," Julia offered.

"But what about you? You've been working all night, aren't you tired too?"

"I'm tired, but I'm not drained. I could give you healing now and it wouldn't be any trouble at all. The healing energy passes through me, it is not of me." Mary wanted to accept, yet she held back.

"I'm not sure. Does it matter if I don't understand all this?"

"All you need to do is to lie back and relax as much as you are able. I'm going to work with my hands either on or near to you, feeding healing energy to the whole of your being as I go. Try to let go of your logic and see what happens."

Mary sighed and lay back. Part of her felt rather foolish and called upon her to pull herself together. After all, how could someone waving their hands about make any difference to her? But there she lay, waiting and feeling rather as she had when Palmer first mentioned that Mandrake's name was Birch - a sense of purpose. This was her adventure.

As Julia worked, Mary's mind ran on in all directions. From time to time, she remembered to relax anew. She saw a clear blue before her eyes. The sun was shining again, then. She must get out for a walk by the sea today and take a break from the hospital. Then she realised that her eyes were shut and that this beautiful blue was in her mind's eye. She had thought, somehow, that she had been staring out of a window, but when she peeped momentarily, she was looking up at the cream coloured ceiling with a dusty smoke alarm set in it.

Mary was intrigued. She could see Julia kneeling on the floor beside her as she held her hands about a foot from her body with her eyes closed. When Mary shut hers again, the blue returned. She felt a warmth within her that was deeply relaxing, joyful.

When she had finished, Julia blessed her. Mary cringed inwardly, yet at the same time, she liked it.

"If you rest for a few minutes and take things as gently as you can today, it will benefit you all the more," Julia said. "I'm going home now. I don't expect to be in again this week, but you never know. What are you going to do? Will you be staying with your brother all the time?"

"How long will he be here do you think? He's an addict. Getting him through this is going to take time."

"Who can say how it will go? Now that he has a sister to support him, someone who really cares, he is in a completely different space to the one he was in only a few days ago. Taking one day at a time is a good way to go forward, especially at a time like this. It's overwhelming to try to work it all out in advance. How do any of us know what lies before us? We're all inventing our lives as we go along. Any amount of planning can't put life in a corset! I must go. Good bye for now."

Mary, reclining on her makeshift bed, followed Julia with her eyes. For the first time in a long time, she thought of the woman she had seen swimming in the quarry, all those years ago.

"I'm on to something," she thought.

CHAPTER SEVENTY-ONE

Letting Go

While Mary was away, Clive and Bruce muddled through their days, juggling the needs of Pascal and Jenny with work commitments. They didn't even try to do it properly with fresh vegetables at routine mealtimes, bed making or dusting. They simply let it happen.

The weather was hot. The children ran around in bare feet, their food-marked tee shirts and dirty shorts delighting them. Mr Croft had not made contact and Bruce gave school no further thought. Everyone was enjoying the change which really did feel as good as a rest.

The more engrossed Clive became in the Mosaic household, the more pleasant his life became. At night, he had a series of joyful dreams in which he was reunited with Zorcia. As the days went by, he became convinced that he must find her again if the rest of his life was to add up to anything worthwhile. He didn't want to be on hold any more. The trouble was, where on earth was he to look? Many years had passed since he had let her go and she had been whisked away from him. She could be anywhere in the world. He talked to Bruce about it.

"I've got to find her."

"Clive, I hear what you say, but how in the name of God are you going to do that?"

"Perhaps I should do just that."

"What do you mean?"

"Try praying?" Clive said speculatively. She's probably not in Japan or India. There must be masses of places we can reasonably rule out at this point. She's probably somewhere in Europe. Perhaps she has even returned to her home village, although with the fighting that went on in that part of the world, who knows what that could have led to?"

"Who knows? It's even possible that the chaos of those earlier years has saved her from something worse."

"Bruce, I must find her again. I've got to try. It's the only way to bring meaning back into my life."

"Would it be possible to go back to her village? Would the Salvation Army or the Red Cross be able to help? Where was she left in Titograd?"

"I don't know the answers to any of these questions. I have been in limbo ever since our separation, believing myself to be incapable of solving this problem. Now, as I said, I see that it's what I have to do. Just knowing that feels like the first step."

When he was lying in bed that night, beginning to fall into sleep, Clive heard a young woman's voice inside his head.

"Go to Salzburg," it said. He fell asleep, full of hope.

CHAPTER SEVENTY-TWO

Time To Think

Mary stayed with Mandrake for almost a week. During that time, she did not miss her family. She spoke to them on the telephone every day. She knew that they were all right. She devoted each day to Mandrake, centring her activities around his needs.

She was used to planning her time around the needs of others. This was different. Mary had booked into a bed and breakfast and so she was looked after too. She did not have to do anything for anyone else when she was not with Mandrake. During each day he would have times when he did not need her with him and Mary would wander off to follow her own desires.

She browsed in the shops and bought presents and clothes for herself and her family. She found a book about healing and then enjoyed hours of solitude, sitting reading on a bench in the sunshine, the sea gleaming before her with unlimited time to read and learn.

What she read was akin to what Julia had said. It challenged her and gently, but most firmly, brought her to the realisation that she did not know who she was. She stopped reading to watch people walking by and wondered if they knew who they were.

Mary could describe herself in conventional terms. She was a woman, a wife, a mother and such like, but who was she? Why was she here, doing this? Did everything have meaning? When she actually stopped to think about it, when all the rushing around stopped, was she in fact able to identify a deeper purpose in her life?

"Who am I?" she asked herself, time and time again. "Which part of me is real? What does that part of me want to do? How do I decide things?" Mary found these questions disturbing as well as interesting. Then she asked herself, "How much of what I do is a blind to keep me so distracted that I never have to address these questions?"

She already knew the answer.

CHAPTER SEVENTY-THREE

Homecoming

By Saturday, Mary felt ready to go home. She and Mandrake had been able to talk, despite the fact that his illness and withdrawal were very taxing for him and he became easily tired and distracted. Julia had come in to work one more night shift. She had given Mandrake more healing. The following morning, when he awoke, Mandrake said,

"Mary, I want to be called Robin again. I want to be Robin again. Without family, I was Mandrake, an outsider, uprooted and alone. Robin is allowed to join in. Robin belongs."

"Robin," she said, smiling. "Welcome." That evening she telephoned Bruce.

"Mary, please come home. We're all missing you to a painful degree and now Clive is off on some crazy venture. I don't know what's happening to us all. Surely Mandrake is over the worst now. We need you back with us." Mary could hear desperation in his voice. She rather liked it.

"That's exactly what I was going to tell you. Mandrake is getting better. He will be all right for a bit. He wants to be called Robin now. It's the name he had when he was a little boy. Bruce, we have talked whenever we can and he has told me so much about my birth family. I have a sister too, called Mandy and we're going to try and find her. Something essential to me has fallen into place. It's wonderful. I'll set off tomorrow at about mid-day."

"Thank heavens for that! By the way, Croft has contacted me at last. He is arranging for Pascal to see the county educational psychologist early next term."

"But that's months away!"

"Apparently it's quite quick. I said that the children could go back to school on Monday."

"It's good in a way, but did he say anything about how things will be for the rest of this term?"

"I think that Croft was expecting praise for arranging the appointment so soon. He didn't mention anything else. Let's talk about it when we're back together. We've got tomorrow evening and I'll warn the children that school is on the cards."

"That just says it all, doesn't it?"

"What do you mean?" Bruce asked anxiously, bracing himself for some sort of tirade whilst quickly checking through what he had said for the offending words.

"That we think of school as so dodgy that we have to warn our children!"

"Ahh, I see," Bruce answered, relieved. There was a silence.

"I'll see you tomorrow then. Lots of love to you all. I'm longing to be home."

"I'm longing to have you home. I'll tell the children. They'll be unbearably excited. They've really missed you - we all have." As Mary put down the receiver, she yearned to hold her family again.

CHAPTER SEVENTY-FOUR

Reunion

In Salzburg, Clive walked the streets. Impulsively, he had set off from England the day before, catching a stand-by flight. He had not been out of the United Kingdom for years and he relished the difference. Today, Sunday, many of the shops were shut. After enjoying coffee and delicious Austrian cakes, he walked on.

Towering above the city, the castle invited him. It would be open today, surely. He did not want to take the lift. It was crowded with tourists and his purpose was different. He had said that he was on holiday at passport control. It would have been impossible to say, "I'm here on a hunch. I'm here because of a voice in a waking dream. I'm here looking for my long lost love." He did not want to say it out loud. The thoughts were too deep to be articulated. Clive walked on up the paths. He came to a playground, busy with children being watched by their mothers who sat near-by, talking to one another. A little further down the path were benches in the sun where he went to sit down.

This was the first time that he had taken repose since his arrival. He didn't count last night, having arrived late and by the time he had found somewhere to stay, he was so tired that he had slept beyond dreams. Now he could reflect, but he found that he could not concentrate his mind. All he could do was to feel a powerful mixture of excitement and peace. He liked it. It felt like a flow of life beginning to stir within.

On his side of the park, a great wall supported the lower structures of the castle. It contained arches which were thrown into shadow by the late morning sun. The way he was feeling, he expected to want to focus on the trees, birds and children, not an old wall, but he felt irresistibly drawn to it. As his eyes accommodated the contrasting light, he could just make out the figure of a woman. She was watching him. Was she crying? He couldn't tell for sure.

Then he found himself walking towards her. She turned and tried to walk away. She stumbled against the wall and as she tried to regain her balance, Clive caught up with her. He reached to take her arm. It was thin and insubstantial. He held her arm and although the woman tried to pull away and keep her face hidden, he knew her.

"Zorcia!" he called, his voice choking with joy and fear. She kept her head down, allowing him to keep her near. She stopped pulling away.

For moments, they stood like this. As time passed, they both understood that their long separation was over. Zorcia turned her head a little to the left and could see, floating down towards her, as she reeled it in, the shining ball of her joy. Clive, as he began to take her in his arms, felt his life returning, running through his veins along with his blood.

CHAPTER SEVENTY-FIVE

Fear That Robin May Be A Cuckoo

When Robin was well enough, he went to live with his family. For him and for Mary, this was easy. They had missed out on their siblinghood and were hungry to create it. Pascal and Jenny accepted their new uncle although they were nervous of upsetting him. He seemed quiet and, in fact, was disappointingly boring. They hoped that he would become more interesting when he was better.

They had overheard conversations about Mandrake, the name he used to have. They had overheard them long before they had known that he was their uncle. They could guarantee that when grown-ups spoke in hushed tones and left out words, then there was a great deal more to find out.

Bruce tried to like the situation. In truth, he found it difficult. He had ungenerous thoughts and couldn't stop them. He didn't know where it was going to lead. Here he was with a homeless ex-junkie living in his house which used to be the ex-junkie's house. The ex-junkie also turns out to be the long lost brother of his wife with whom she is spending more time than with him. He could put up with disruption for a while, but not for ever. He wanted his old routine back.

The other worry was Mary's parents, Hugh and Clarissa. They had been unnerved by Robin's arrival, there was no doubt about that. Where did it put them? They said they were happy for Mary and Robin, although he could see that they weren't at ease. They must be worried that the two of them would go on to trace their parents and that would have an effect on Pascal and Jenny. Would they still be grand-parents if the original ones were found? At least he didn't have to worry along those lines. His wife might not notice him much at the moment, but at least the state of her birth and adoptive families couldn't change the fact that they were husband and wife.

With Clive away, Bruce felt he had no one to talk to. He wanted so much to be happy with all of this and he thought that it would be easier if only he could get it all off his chest. So much had happened lately that he felt only Clive would understand. Besides, when he stopped to think, although he had many friends, his relationship with them tended to be rushed and quite shallow. He could not think of anyone with whom he could share all of this. He felt lonely. He would not tell Mary this. He did not want to upset her. He busied himself at work. After all, there was another mouth to feed now.

Into the middle of this, a letter arrived. It was from Clive. He said that he had found Zorcia and was bringing her home. Bruce was awe-struck. He could not believe it. Mary understood.

"It's called going with the flow," she said. "That's the quickest way to find your heart's desire.

CHAPTER SEVENTY-SIX

Multi-dimensional Reunion

Clive brought Zorcia home after he had married her. Radiating joy, he took her to meet the Mosaics. Her face had released its pain and her beauty spoke through the wear of unhappiness. Her smile was utterly engaging. Instead of talking, the friends depended upon nodding and the exchange of gifts and food, with Clive using his rusty German to interpret when needed. Jenny sat between Zorcia and Clive and was content.

Robin arrived later. He was expecting to meet Clive and his new wife and returned to Stonelea ready for a strange reunion with a man who, up to now, he had only known as a hospital porter who had wheeled him about on his frequent former admissions to hospital. Nothing could have prepared him for the impossible reunion that awaited him.

When he entered the room, Robin's first attention was for Clive. They shook hands. Clive greeted him with a warmth that eased Robin immediately. When he turned to be introduced to his new wife, he simply could not believe his eyes.

He had only seen the girl briefly as she had run into the night club, clutching that old chest, before she was taken through to a side room and curtained off. Then he had caught sight of her as she had been slung, unconscious, over a shoulder and taken off by Klimpt. But he was not mistaken. This unusual and lovely woman before him was the same person.

Robin became pale and weak. He felt himself drifting away from the room, his eyes only able to focus on the narrow view before him. He could see her face changing as the ready smile gave way to bewilderment. Robin sat suddenly on the floor. Mary ran to him and helped him to lie down, elevating his feet onto two hastily gathered cushions.

"It's okay," he said weakly. "I can explain. It's another strange event."

Pascal went to get a glass of water. Jenny knelt beside Robin and watched over him, her eyes wide and hinting at tears. Bruce opened a window and Mary a door, creating a through-draft. Clive took Zorcia's hand, reassuring her.

When Robin had taken a small drink and the colour was retuning to his face, he beckoned to Jenny to come closer to him. He whispered to her and she jumped up and ran from the room. He held his hand up to indicate a request for them to bear with him. In the quiet, Jenny's footsteps took her upstairs and ran lightly into Robin's room. Then came the sound of a drawer being opened, a short pause and then she ran back.

"I've got it, Uncle Robin!" she called, waving a small, very grubby rag as she entered the room.

"Here Jenny, give it to me," said Robin. He took it from her swiftly and made it disappear inside his hand. "Thanks," he said and then began to tell his story. When he described the moment when he had seen the handkerchief fall from Zorcia's pocket, he unfolded his hand, opened out the handkerchief and there, in the corner, was the mark that Clive had made all those years ago just before Zorcia and he were separated.

Robin offered it to Zorcia and Clive. They took it in amazement, staring at it together as Zorcia smoothed it out on to her lap.

"What was the chest like?" asked Jenny. Robin had seen even less of the chest than he had of Zorcia on that dreadful night. The whole incident had left such a deep impression on him that what details he had observed had stayed with him. He could remember its size, its shape and the padlock swinging from its clasp, so when he had described these things, Jenny said, "We've got one like that in our attic."

"I can't take much more of this!" said Bruce.

"It's got to be," said Mary, full of wonder and excitement. As soon as Robin was well enough, they all went upstairs.

Bruce opened the trap door and arranged the steps. One by one, they climbed the ladder into the attic and then walked carefully across the beams. Pascal was the last as he had run off to find a torch. At the far end of the attic, Jenny parted the rail of clothes and pointed to the chest. Pascal, catching his breath, pointed his torch. Zorcia and Robin stared at it in further amazement.

"That's a spitting image of it if it's not the same," said Robin.

Zorcia knelt down beside it. After all these years, she could not mistake it. The shape, size and colour were identical and so was the padlock. She looked up at Clive and then at all of them.

"Yes," she said. "This yes," as she nodded at Robin.

"What's inside?" asked Jenny.

"That's what we'd all like to know. And how did it get here? Do you know how it got here Robin? I'm assuming from your reaction that it's not something you left behind knowingly," said Bruce.

"It was never here when I was," Mandrake replied. "I left to find it. It doesn't add up at all."

"The house was open when we arrived to move in," said Mary. "The door was hanging open. There were leaves blowing up the hallway. We've always assumed that that was how you left it Robin." He was thoughtful, trying to remember for sure.

"I left unhappily. You know the state I was in. I didn't know what I was doing half the time. It could've easily been left unlocked."

"Then something happened between your departure and our arrival," said Bruce. "Someone brought this chest here during that time, though heaven knows why. Come on, let's get it downstairs and solve the mystery. Do I take it that none of us knows what it contains? Bruce went to pick it up. It was heavy. Zorcia brushed past him and tried to lift it.

"Me...er...er.." She mimed herself being able to pick it up with ease, that it had not been so heavy when she had had to carry it, talking to Clive as she did so and he confirmed Zorcia's meaning.

"Come on, Clive!" Bruce said, "this is a two man job now, especially up here in this awkward space. If everyone else goes on down, we'll do our best to bring it with us."

When Bruce and Clive had put the chest on the sitting room floor, everyone gathered round. Bruce knelt down and examined the padlock.

"That's extraordinary," he said. "There's no keyhole. How on earth do we get into this?" He pulled at it tentatively to see if it would open. Then he gave it a jerk. There was no give. Zorcia spoke to Clive.

"Zorcia says this is the same lock as before," he said. "But she never opened it." In turn, each adult made their exploration of this mystery. No one could budge it and neither could they prise open the chest in any other way. It seemed to be sealed.

"I'm going to cut through the hinges," said Bruce and went to fetch his hack-saw.

"No, wait!" said Mary. Bruce halted impatiently and turned to her.

"What do you suggest then?" he challenged.

"I don't know. I just feel bad about the idea of damaging it." Bruce sighed with exasperation and carried on.

Seeing and understanding his mother's distress, Pascal crouched beside the chest. He took the padlock in his hands, wondering at this puzzle that the grown-ups could not solve. As he held it, noting its smooth inscrutability, he wished that he could open it and bring his mother joy. As he longed for this outcome, holding the lock tightly, he felt it so strongly that, for a glorious moment, it seemed possible. His father reappeared with his tool box. The small group, reluctant but cowed, stepped back to let him pass. Pascal braced himself to stand, his heart beginning to sink after its sudden soaring vision of him as saviour and he let go of the lock. It sprung open with his hand.

"Look at that!" exclaimed Clive, "Pascal's done it!".

"How did you do that?" Bruce asked. Jenny edged close to Pascal. She felt proud of him. Mary's eyes filled with tears amidst the general rejoicing. It was Zorcia who was drawn to open it. With Clive kneeling beside her and the family gathered near by, Zorcia, her hands trembling, raised the lid.

There was a stoneware jar. It was sealed with wax. When they opened it, it was full of sand. There was a dark glass bottle sealed with a cork and inside, a liquid that looked like water. A large wooden box was inlaid with a design of the sun. Inside, there was a host of iridescent and multi-coloured feathers. At the bottom of the chest there was a letter. It was from Klara.

My Dear Friends,

Finding this letter means that you have found one another. It means that you have trusted yourselves in new ways and found it to be fruitful. It means that the work that I have been doing to support each of you in your search, is now complete. You have found representations of the five elements: Earth, Water, Fire, Air and Ether, this last being also the first that goes unseen and yet binds each one of us to the other. They contain the energy of nature, the energy of the Universe. Are you dissociated from them or are you aligned with them?

I ask each one of you to reflect on the events of recent weeks and, in that light, to address these questions:

Who am I? What is my truth? Why do I live the way I do?

And I ask you this,

Do any of you desire to look at and to know yourselves completely? Now that you have found one another, is it time to find yourselves? Are you ready?

Bliss, joy, peace and love await to fill your hearts for all time - and so it is.

Klara.

CHAPTER SEVENTY-SEVEN

Mary Swims Free

Sitting high on her quarry rock, Mary smiles as she completes her recollection, contrasting the person she is now with the ignorant young woman of years ago who had been willing to trade the adventure of love for the supposed security of hiding herself. What a lot she has missed. It is sad, but she will not allow that to diminish her life any more. It has all brought her to here, now and she is ready to leap.

Mary stands up. The water invites her. It looks like a long drop. "I'm either in, or I'm not," she says to herself. Then she says, "Go on Mary, show your self, your self!". She jumps through the sunlight and into the water. She does not want to float quietly. She is too ecstatic. She kicks her legs, splashing her way through the water and blinkingly watching it cascade all around her. Weightless, supported, liberated, she has found her way.

It is better to know how to love
Than how to behave

The next book to be
published by Fairmead Press
will be
Leaving The Cult
by
Joy Buchanan

Fairmead Press

Panborough, Wells, Somerset. BA5 1PN
www.fairmeadlife.co.uk